Books by J. Alexander Greenwood:

Pilate's Cross
Pilate's Cross: The Audiobook
Pilate's Key
Pilate's Ghost
Pilate's Blood

Non-Fiction:

Kickstarter Success Secrets
Kickstarter Success Secrets: The Audiobook

Most books available in paperback and ebook formats wherever books are sold.

PILATE'S BLOOD

Thicker Than Water. Twice As Deadly.

John Pilate Mysteries Book Four

A Caroline Street Press Book

J. Alexander Greenwood

Cover designed by Scarlett Rugers Design www.scarlettrugers.com

ISBN: 978-0-9883201-4-7 (sc)
ISBN: 978-0-9883201-3-0 (e)

Lulu Publishing Services rev. date: 02/12/2015

Dedicated to Everyone
Who's Been
A Jack
to
A King
and Back

Contents

Prologue

Hell is surely hot, thought Alvin as the sweat ran down his face, chest, and the middle of his powerful, blacksmith's back. The light from the lantern was poor, but his weary eyes knew well enough what he would see: dirt, rock, roots, and darkness.

Dank and dark, like a welldigger's arsehole.

He was almost finished, but that gave him only a small modicum of relief. The box he had secreted for Jubal Olafson wasn't safe above ground. Word had come on last week's stage stop in Cross Camp that the canny son-of-a-bitch, Ballanger, and his pard, Cotton Johnson, were looking for something important, and this time it was more than Frank Tash's $60,000 in stolen herd money. The pair had made short work of Monte Crandall and his brothers, Reed and Hoyte. Hell, Monte even got his neck stretched for his trouble.

Hunting down stolen money wasn't Ballanger and Cotton's primary vocation, but word on the trail was that they were up for just about anything, as long as the price was right. Alvin wasn't taking any chances.

If Ballanger and Cotton rode up from Indian Territory to sniff the air, they'd reckon pretty damn quick who Jubal's blacksmith was. They'd turn their hairy nostrils to sniffing around his smithy and find the box.

Alvin wasn't a saint, himself, but he sure hated that Jubal took that looted rebel box at the expense of three men's lives. The Swede had smiled and smiled like true villains do, helping Alvin haul the heavy box off his wagon and into the smithy. Under a thin veneer of trail dust, the box was stained dark with blood.

"Those retired Johnny Rebs. Ha! They's got blood as red as da dirt back in Ind'in territ'try," Jubal said, laughing and wiping his thick neck with a filthy handkerchief.

"Kilt?" Alvin asked, not looking Jubal in the eye.

“They didn’t surrender when we admonished them to do so, so…well, we introduced ’em to their God, and I do not mean the revered General Lee. Took the lockbox and put the licks in to get back across the Missouri. Course, I had to remove a couple saddle bums from my employ when all da shoutin’ was done. Not trustworthy, see, men who’d kill so easy.”

Concern creased Alvin’s features.

“Al, you got nothin’ to fear.” Jubal laughed again. “We been square for years. Trust means all, my friend.”

Alvin nodded. “So… What do you want me to do with the box?”

“Just keep it safe here in the smithy, till I get back from Fort Kearney,” he said, resting a meaty hand on Alvin’s anvil. “There’s a lovely piece of Calico up there in Yagmin’s Saloon. I suspect she’d enjoy my attention to her prat.”

Alvin mentally brushed off Jubal’s vulgarity and shifted the heavy box with a groan.

“Here, man. Don’t rupture yourself,” he said, rising to aid the blacksmith.

“It’s damn heavy.”

The men muscled the box behind a coal-fired forge in the corner of the smithy and covered it with a tarpaulin.

“When you comin’ back?”

“Gimme a fortnight or so,” Jubal said, picking his impressive nose and eating what he found. He then ran a filthy hand through his blond, Nordic locks. “I need a bath. May head over to Feather’s tent. She performs quite the old-fashion.”

Jubal turned to leave, laying a filthy finger beside his nose rather than in it. “Alvin, uh… There’s one more thing.”

“Yes, Jubal?”

“Don’t get no ideas ’bout that box. You’ll be rewarded if I return to find it safe and sound. On the contrary, if I return and it’s been disturbed…well, no dark corner of Hell will be far enough out of reach of my hand.” Jubal held his meaty hand out to Alvin, as if for a shake. Then, instead, he curled it into a greasy fist, pulled it away, winked, and strode into the thoroughfare.

* * *

Alvin sat up at night in his smithy, a double-barreled shotgun at the ready as he watched over the cursed box. He waited a fortnight, then another, then another, with no sign of Jubal.

Eventually, word arrived in Cross Camp that Jubal Olafson had been brutally stabbed to death back at Fort Kearney, in the midst of a passionate embrace, no less. The lovely piece of Calico at Yagmin's apparently had other ideas rather than allowing Jubal to sodomize her.

Alvin eyed a pickaxe in the opposite corner of the smithy, a relic obtained on barter with a prospector for some horseshoes. He pondered a moment about swinging it down on the bloody box lock. Instead, he spat on the floor, put aside the shotgun, picked up the pickaxe, and swung with all his might into the soft Nebraska earth.

Chapter One

A haze of cigar smoke gave the tiny room a Beijing-in-winter sort of look. It was the kind of place where factories pumped out sticky soot you'd find tattooed under your collar after a three-minute walk around the block.

"Two," Hilmer Thurman said, working the word out from around a stub of cigar.

Nelda, a willing victim of forty years lying prone in a tanning bed, dealt two cards.

"I'll take three," Robeson said, holding up three dark fingers for emphasis.

The leathery Nelda dutifully dealt three cards.

"Off the top of the deck, if ya don't mind." Robeson's pearly teeth shone in the haze.

A chorus of masculine laughter ensued around the table as the men belched out smoke with their chuckles.

Thurman allowed a faint grin and glanced "Ya know our Nelda better than that, Robeson," he said, his mouth curling a grin around the cigar.

"Yeah, ya asshole," Nelda said, laughing, her crow's feet deepening.

"Just teasin'," Robeson said, pushing his trucker cap back on his sweaty head and scrubbing at his thinning curls.

"Shit, I know, Robie," Nelda said. She flung cards at the other two men at the table after they signaled their next moves. "Everybody still in?" she asked, her long, garish nails tapping the felt.

Everyone nodded.

"Okay," she said. "Here's the river."

"Things sure been quiet 'round here lately," Robeson said, scratching absently at his chin.

Thurman grunted, his eyes on his cards, his face sans smile.

A young, sinewy man with wide, weed-weary eyes farted. "'Scuse."

"Otis, please!" Nelda said, rolling heavily shadowed eyes.

"That sure as hell wasn't quiet," Parker Nemec said, waggling his eyebrows. The youngest man at the table, he was president of the tiny but solvent Bank of Cross. "Sounds like Otis had some o' your baked beans with his burnt ends today."

Robeson grunted and threw a ten-spot in the pot. "Ma beans do not tend toward da gassy, for your information."

"Yeah, right," Nemec said. "Well, I gotta say your ribs are fantastic. What do ya put on 'em? Some kinda dry rub?"

Long a local institution, Bart Robeson's Tin Roof Rib Shack set just off the state highway, a few miles from Thurman's Brown Betty Roadhouse. Southeastern Nebraska wasn't particularly known for high-quality, not-to-be-missed barbecue, making the Shack an oasis for barbecue fiends. Unlike the repulsive soot belched by Chinese factories, the Tin Roof Rib Shack's sweet smoke drew locals and out-of-towners alike, seemingly against their will.

"Secret recipe," Robeson said, his gravelly voice somewhere between a whisper and a mumble.

"We talkin' or playin'?" Thurman said, good-natured but betraying a mounting impatience.

"Good hand there, Hils?" Nemec surmised.

Thurman shot him a brief, stony look, to which Nemec responded with a nervous laugh.

Otis unleashed a second gaseous issue, which reverberated like sharp raps on a solid oak door. "'Scuse," he recited again.

"Oh good God," Nelda said.

"That, my friend, is inexcusable," Nemec said. "I bet fifty."

"You ain't ma friend," Otis mumbled, his bloodshot eyes on his cards.

Nemec shrugged, aiming for nonchalance, though he felt a creeping unease in the wake of Otis's callous remark, especially after Thurman's cold eye. "Okay," he said, keeping his eyes on the prize.

Thurman bet fifty, plus twenty more.

Robeson glanced from his cards to the orange tip of his cigar, and then his eyes drifted lazily to the pot. He produced a wad of cash from his pocket and thumbed a wrinkled c-note on the table.

Nemec whistled through the gap in his front teeth.

Thurman puffed on his stogie, his lip curling on the left side. "I think--"

"A hundert?" Otis said. "Shit! You know I don't carry that much--"

"Then fold, negro," Robeson said, smiling.

Otis blinked, twice. "You don't gotta be like dat."

Thurman glanced over Nemec's shoulder, staring at Tom. "Everything goin' all right, buddy?"

Tom nodded and adjusted his trucker cap, then folded hairy, meaty arms across his barrel chest and belly. He gestured to Nelda with his chin.

"A man of few words," Nemec observed.

Otis sighed, then jammed his index finger in his mouth. He dug around until a popping sound issued, and then he tossed his teeth on the pot. "There," he said through his gums. "Dem dentures is wert five hundert, easy."

"Good Lord, man, maybe to you they are," Nemec said.

"Oh yeah, dat car wreck took your natural choppers." Robeson cackled. "A'ight. I'll cover ya, but if you lose, you're gonna wash those things in Bud before I take 'em."

"Good idea. Nelda, can you get me another beer?" Thurman said.

"My pleasure. Anybody else?" As she stood, she banged her head on the single naked light bulb suspended over the table, the tiny room's only source of illumination. "Ow! Damn it." She steadied the bulb with one hand, rubbing her head with the other. "Can you gents handle this? I think I need a drink and a smoke or three after two farts and an upper in the pot."

Thurman nodded. "We're about through here anyway."

She nodded, then squeezed past the men to head to the door, her exit letting foul air out and country music in.

Thurman chuckled softly. "So, Parker, I hear your bank swooped in on Perry Mostek's widow pretty fast."

"Swooped in?"

"Well, yeah. He only disappeared what? Three, four months before you turned up as Perry's wife's business agent. Your bank wants to auction the property off to the highest bidder."

"Well, that's business. Mrs. M. came to us, and Perry probably ain't coming back," Nemec said, his eyes on his cards, a bead of sweat tickling his right armpit.

"Maybe, maybe not. Yet you decided you'd quietly entertain an offer on one of the last going concerns in this one-horse town without so much as a by-your-leave reach-around for the rest of us?"

"Well, I…uh… The Mosteks are struggling, and the town needs a store. I figured you'da said something if you wanted it before now, so--"

"I hear that Mick B&B owner put up an offer. He's no grocer. What the hell does he want with it?"

"He says his family ran pubs and grocery shops back in Cork, in Ireland," Nemec stammered. "His bed-and-breakfast has done real well. He wants to diversify his portfolio."

"Well, tough shit," Thurman said.

Robeson kept his eyes on the table.

"That kind of shit bothers me, Parker," Thurman said, puffing on his cigar, his forehead wrinkled in consternation. "Know why?"

Nemec shook his head. His hands trembled, and moisture leeched into his cards. He was as pissed as he was scared. He wasn't used to the rough stuff; in the past, his position with the bank and a need to appear to be above the board made him immune to such behavior.

"Because my cousin, Ollie, used to run this town. You took your marchin' orders from him till that idiot, Scovill, and his boy wonder pal, Pontius Pilate, blew him and Craig away."

"Now, Hilmer," he said, raising a finger, "You never… You never expressed any interest in the store, so I--"

"I guess people think they can get away with murder around here, maybe worse."

"You bet. I think you've got that part of Ollie's portfolio covered." Nemec smiled but regretted the misfired attempt at flattery even before the last syllable took flight.

Thurman nodded, and Tom, moving with surprising alacrity for a large man in such a tight space, wrapped a length of wire around Nemec's neck and began to twist it.

Nemec's eyes bulged, his complexion blotchy as he rose from his chair, grunting and clawing at Tom's massive paws.

Otis and Robeson sat motionless, except for Robeson's cigar, which fell from his limp mouth, rolled down his ample shirtfront, and collided with the floor in a hail of sparks.

Thurman leaned forward, removed the cigar stub from his mouth, and blew smoke in Nemec's slowly strangling face. "Got a few breathin' problems, eh?"

Nemec did his best to nod, his hands clawing at Tom's.

"So we've got your attention?"

A blob of spittle fell from his lips, and tears worked from his eyes as he tried to nod again.

"I say what's what in this shitty little town. *You bet,*" Thurman said. His voice never rose or quavered; it was as if he was casually explaining what cards were wild in the next hand. "Not you, not Robie or Otis or that new college president bitch, and especially not that asshole, John Pilate. You got that?" He paused, as if to let it sink in, then continued, "Now, you're gonna do me a favor, and I'll return one. *Comprende*?"

Tom's grip on Nemec loosened.

Nemec nodded, gagging and choking.

When Nemec caught his breath, Thurman resumed. "You're gonna cancel the deal with the widow, and you'll recommend that Mrs. Mostek call me and take my offer. You're gonna tell Cusack the deal's off, that Mostek changed her mind. Then you're gonna keep your mouth shut. Got it?"

Again, a nod attempt.

"Good, because if you don't, if you screw up even one of those things, big Tom here will twist your head off, and Robie'll smoke your ass and serve the carcass to family and friends at your wake."

Robie's gaze scraped the table, his hands clutching his cards.

Otis snickered into his fist, until Thurman raised an eyebrow.

Tom pulled Nemec to his feet.

Nemec gurgled, gagging some more.

"Good." Thurman nodded, and Tom let go of the wire.

Nemec fell forward on the poker table. His right arm flailed, smashing the light bulb. The room fell into darkness, save the orange glow of Hilmer Thurman's cigar cherry. Nemec gasped, heaved, and gurgled then sank to the floor.

"Damn your eyes, Otis. Don't even think of making a grab for your fucking teeth," Thurman said. "This hand ain't over."

Chapter Two

"What do you mean, *gone*?" Pilate said, clutching the phone in a white-knuckled grip and pacing in his farmhouse kitchen.

"He left," Monique Fraley said, her voice squirming with the slippery finality of an unpleasant truth.

"With *my* money?" Pilate said, stifling the urge to shout. He glanced out the window at his wife, Kate, his stepdaughter, Kara, and his infant son, Peter, playing in oak leaves piled in mounds around the yard.

"Well, the bank accounts are cleaned out, which means he eloped with money from every author in his stable," Fraley said, her words tinged with a resigned disgust, "and my last two paychecks."

"I'm sorry, Monique," Pilate said. "My book was a bestseller. Six weeks or whatever on the list and we've hardly seen a dime. If Frechette skipped town, does that mean we may never see that money?"

"I know it seems that way, John." The publicist sighed. "But it's not like he took your book too. You'll see whatever future proceeds the book earns."

"But it fell off the bestseller list. The real money's done coming in, right? I mean, how will the book have distribution without a publisher?"

She sighed again. "Well, that's where it gets...tricky. We need to seek some sort of injunctive relief and block Frechette from accessing any future earnings. Then we put the paperback rights and your future output up for auction. I'm thinking another publisher will be happy to snatch you up."

"Thanks. I appreciate that, but what you're telling me is that, for the foreseeable future, I'm screwed. Could be months."

"More like one or two years."

"Shit," he whispered. "I was *this* close to getting outta here, moving the whole family somewhere that isn't teeming with blood and shit."

"I know, John," she said. "What does your agent say? Angee?"

"Oh, her. Miss Thing can't even be bothered to pick up her phone. As soon as this all started, she dumped me, said she needs to refocus her attention on higher-earning clientele. That two-faced…" He paused to take a frustrated sigh of his own. "I'd like to smash those damn glasses she's always chewing on, trying to look smart."

Monique clicked her tongue. "Tsk tsk. And they say publicists are the a-holes."

"What about you? What're you gonna do?"

"Well…" she breathed out, her tone dropping conspiratorially. "I'm working at another couple houses, doing publicity, but I think what I really wanna do is become an agent."

"Good Lord, why? After all this? Besides, what about eBooks?"

"What about 'em? Ebooks won't replace the big publishers overnight, and I have a hot new talent just waiting for a good agent and a better deal."

"Hmm. Well, I hope this hot new talent's got a good book up her sleeve," he said, shifting the lace curtain back, turning his family into three gauzy figures moving on the grass.

"Well, now that you mention it, I wanted to ask if you have anything new in the pipeline?"

"Huh?"

"A follow-up to *Murder 101*?"

"Oh. Well, I've been thinking about--"

Monique snickered.

"Wait. You're talking about…me? *I'm* your hot new talent?"

"Well, let's qualify that. *You,* personally, are *not* hot, in my humble opinion, but your temp in the publishing world is higher than lukewarm, and you seem to need a good agent, so…"

Pilate laughed. "Well, it also seems I need to make some money, pronto. You're hired."

"All right. The deal is 20 percent and a piece of film rights," she said.

"Eighteen."

She clicked her tongue. "Okay."

"Okay, fine. Nevertheless, I could use a sizeable advance. I have to go back to teaching now. I need money to make my daring daylight escape from the town that time forgot."

"Would you be willing to do short pieces? Magazines and such?"

"I'll take it, even *Hustler* if I have to."

"Ew."

"I'm serious, Monique. I don't care, as long as the checks will clear."

"Let's not get desperate so quickly, okay? I'll overnight a contract to you. I'll also get started with a lit attorney I know, see about emancipating your book from Frechette and severing your relationship with Angee."

"A simple 'screw you' would be fitting, and I can't afford a bloodsucking attorney," Pilate said with a snort.

"Especially in conjunction with your psychiatry bills," Simon said from a comfortable spot somewhere in Pilate's cranium. For most of his life, Pilate had harbored Simon, his emotionally jaundiced, acerbic inner voice, confidant, and occasional tormenter.

"He'll work cheap."

"Monique, cheap attorneys are like cheap doctors, more dangerous than doing it yourself."

"Look, if he doesn't give me a good deal, he won't get that special thing I do with a repeated flick of my wrist on Friday nights," she said, her lips curling audibly through the receiver.

"What thing? Oh. I see. So he's a--"

"A friend...and that's all you need to know, old man."

"Well, I'm all for friendship."

"Gross." She chuckled.

"Okay. Well, thanks for the help, Monique...and the hope," Pilate said. "I'll start thinking about the next book. The serial killer stuff would be a good follow-up, but a lot of what happened in Florida is off the table."

"Why? That's probably the juiciest bit," she said.

"You're right, sort of. The juiciest bit is actually between me and--"

"That chickie cop you did the bed sheet shuffle with?"

"Never you mind, young lady. I'm actually talking about the offshore stuff. I'm legally forbidden from sharing what happened out in the Gulf, but I'll think of something. A good writer can fill in plot holes nicely, right?"

"Well, unless you did the cop out on the boat, we need to act now, Mr. Handcuffs Fetish," she said. "Can you get me a proposal in two weeks?"

"Two weeks? As in only fourteen days? Holy shit."

"I'm not asking you to write the whole book," she said. "Just need a proposal so I can get you that fat advance and my 20 percent."

Pilate sagged against the kitchen counter. "Monique…"

"Yeah?"

"How much of my money do you think Frechette has?"

"Oh, probably around $632,481.21."

"That mother--"

"Gotta go. Get crackin' on that proposal, and I'll get moving on everything else. Bye, lover." She loosed a dirty laugh and hung up.

Pilate put the old receiver back on the wall. When his children's laughter wafted through the screen door, he glanced again at the small patio area he had built, complete with a fancy little Weber Smoky Mountain smoker that bore a resemblance to R2-D2. A few yards beyond, on the edge of the ecotone between the yard and cornfields, rose an ancient oak that gave the best shade.

"October's comin' up fast," Simon said.

"Yep. Time to get a job."

* * *

"What's with that old door in the barn?" Pilate asked over a late breakfast.

"That old slab of oak?" Kate asked quietly, holding her infant close to her breast. "It used to be the front door here, back when Rick and I first bought the place. It's pretty but not as secure or energy efficient as we wanted, so we got the new fiberglass one and the tacky storm door."

"Ya know, it'd make a great bar, under the oak tree."

"What?"

"Well, I get tired of standing around the back yard when I need some time to myself. I want a place to relax."

"We have Adirondack chairs, honey."

"I like to lean, not sit."

"You just wanna drink in the back yard at your own bar. Is that it?" she asked with a smirk.

"And what's wrong with that?"

"Nothing. You know, if you want to make it into a bar, we can put a canopy over it and hang some tiki lights."

"Tiki lights?"

"Well, yeah…so you can be out there at night."

"Let's not get too precious, dear," he said. Sensing he was losing her, he added, "But okay. I guess tiki lights would be fine. We can use citronella, keep the bugs away."

Kate was glad to hear that her husband now had a project to take his mind off losing the book royalties. To Kate, John Pilate seemed perpetually preoccupied, as if he was keeping company with other voices inside him. *Perhaps a project will quiet whatever is disturbing him so much,* she hoped. "Great," she said, "but that door's heavy. Make sure you get some help with it."

"Okay."

"What are you gonna call it?"

"The bar?"

She nodded.

"The Frontdoor Backyard Bar sounds about right," Simon said.

"The Frontdoor Backyard Bar sounds about right," Pilate parroted.

Kate's face brightened. "Hmm. I like it." She made a face and scrunched up her nose. "Phew! Somebody just made a doody."

"Wasn't me." Pilate raised a newspaper in defense.

"You take him," Kate said.

"Where's Kara? Let her do it."

"She's with her grandpa, remember? They're at that OakFest planning meeting."

"Grif took his seven-year-old granddaughter to a planning meeting for the most boring community festival in history?"

Kate shrugged. "She loves spending time with him, no matter what they're doing." She pushed Peter toward Pilate's newspaper.

The stinky infant swatted at it.

"Okay, my poopy little man, let's go," Pilate said, dropping the paper and taking his son to the nursery. "Daddy's gonna build us a bar!"

Chapter Three

"I started out as a master plumber," Dean Don Felix said, leaning back in his chair, an expansive smile peeling thin lips from his teeth. "There are three things you learn right away as a plumber. Shit rolls downhill, payday is Friday, and never, ever bite your fingernails." He chuckled softly, extending his index finger.

Pilate managed a smile, though it didn't match that of the new dean's. The former plumber was the polar opposite of his friend, the late Dean Peter Trevathan. Trevathan was old; Felix was relatively young, barely knocking on fifty's door. Trevathan was silver-haired, lean, crusty, and had a bark of cranky where his skin should've been; Felix was round, balding, and exuded the unctuous mien of an insurance salesman.

Where Trevathan favored plaid flannel shirts, Felix wore a short-sleeved button-down, with a polyester Ex Libris tie. Trevathan's office, once replete with Western memorabilia, books, and hunting trophies, now displayed textbooks, a collection of small, die-cast metal cars, and photos of Felix and people Pilate presumed were family, though Pilate noted that the man was not wearing a wedding band.

Trevathan suffered fools poorly, but as much as it went against Pilate's psychotherapy to make snap judgments about people, he had already decided that the new dean was leaning toward fool. *Trevathan's ghost must give Felix the finger often,* Pilate thought.

"So… I was a master plumber for eight years, and I get called in to unclog a ladies' locker room toilet at UNO one day. Disgusting what girls try to flush." He made a face. "Anyway, I decided right then and there that I missed being in college. I wanted to be back among the ivy-covered halls of academe."

Simon snickered.

"So you flushed away a successful career in the porcelain arts for all this?" Pilate said, looking around the room and gesturing to the oval outside the window.

Felix didn't catch the sarcasm Pilate had lobbed, one-handed over the plate. "Yep," he said, another fool's strike. "I went back to school and earned my PhD in history. Did my dissertation on Lewis and Clark. I ended up teaching for about ten years before I moved up the ranks at a couple small colleges in Iowa and South Dakota."

"So this is your first, um…deanship?" Pilate asked, fighting to stay interested.

"Ha! Well, yes, I guess, but I'm excited to be here at Cross," he said, gazing out the window. "So much history here, though there's been a little too much drama lately, as you well know." Dean Felix's eyes moved from the window that overlooked the quad, and he turned his gaze on Pilate. His brow knitted together, his smile frozen on a fat head cocked to the side.

Pilate was fully aware of the recent drama. He'd been the leading man in the performance, after all.

Pilate first appeared on campus almost two years prior, as a sad-sack instructor, freshly divorced and full of self-loathing. He stumbled upon a conspiracy that spanned the decades since JFK was shot, narrowly survived attempts on his life, and wrote a bestselling book about the entire affair.

Then, the indicted former president of Cross College lost his marbles and tried to kill Pilate, his family, and Trevathan, the former dean. Somewhere in the midst of all that, Pilate partied hard in Key West, married Kate, and adopted a stepdaughter. Mere months earlier, Kate and Pilate welcomed a son, Peter, Trevathan's namesake, but the dean died of cancer shortly thereafter.

"Drama indeed," said Simon.

"Yes, well, that's all done now, Dean," Pilate said. "Peace, quiet, and boredom has found its way back to Cross College."

"Of course," Felix said, leaning forward, clasping his fingers in front of him on Trevathan's old desk. "And that's just what we want. Our new president is intent on getting this school out of the tabloids." He held a hand up to Pilate. "Sorry. Didn't mean it like that. Poor choice of words, but I'm sure you know what I mean. We need to get back in the business of being a great school, not a magnet for headlines, sensationalism, and criminality."

Pilate matched the dean's gesture with one of his own. "Couldn't agree more."

"So..."

"So?" Pilate coaxed.

"What are your plans?" he asked, again with the insurance salesman's smile.

"Well, I'm through flogging my book, and--"

"Congrats, by the way. A bestseller, I hear."

Pilate nodded. "Yes, and now my wife and I--"

"Wonderful instructor, Kate. So glad she's going to stay with us."

Pilate swallowed, growing frustrated by the interruptions. "Yes. Well, she's a teacher. That's her love."

"She was missed during her maternity leave and the car accident," he said, chewing on the cap of a ballpoint pen. "Sorry. Bad habit." He put the gnarled plastic cap on his desk.

"Well, it's apparently better than chewing your nails."

"Heh. Right. Okay, since she's staying, does this mean you want to resume your class load?"

Pilate's stomach churned. The answer was a resounding no, as in *"Hell no, Dean Felix...and fuck you very much."* He wanted to get back to his simple life again, if that was possible. Teaching could do that, but he would prefer to have the book money and a shot at life in a new place with his family.

"I miss the ocean," Simon said.

"Well, I'm interested in teaching a couple sections, if you'll have me," Pilate said, shrugging.

"Atta boy," Felix said, his smile bursting from his cheeks again. "We can get you back into speech and comp. Sound good?"

Pilate nodded.

"How about spring session?"

"Spring?" Pilate swallowed. "That's almost four months away."

"Well, yes," Felix said, "but we've already found subs for your other classes. We have to honor those contracts. Perhaps we could see if we offer a section with you as instructor… Hmm. Maybe online. Yes, if we could get twenty students to sign up, then we could bring you in sooner."

The wages for one section would be barely enough to make a couple mortgage payments. Pilate nodded though, having lost any will to speak.

"Just one more thing." The dean's smile evaporated. "No more interviews."

"I'm sorry?"

"Well, once you're back on the payroll, the president wants all the Cross College tragedy stuff to go away. She said no more interviews, no more press. You said you're finished promoting your book anyway, so that's it for the media, okay?"

Pilate stifled his desire to tell him to screw off, not because he disagreed but mostly because he didn't like anyone--least of all that dollar-store Ned Beatty--telling him what to do. He inhaled, filling the lower lobes of his lungs, where he imagined smoke from his cigarette-smoking days still hibernated.

"I understand. No problem. Shit rolls downhill, right? But what do I do if the media calls? Just hang up?"

"Well, if you need somebody to play bad cop, just send them over to the PR office. Let that guy earn his pay," Felix said.

"Hmm. The media will think it a little strange that I suddenly can't speak to them. I'm no PR guy, but that could be a PR nightmare all its own."

Felix had a look on his face that reminded Pilate of his stepdaughter, Kara, trying to work out a tough math equation in her head. He scrunched his brow, screwed up his mouth, and looked up to his right, then blew air from his crimson cheeks. "Okay," he finally said, "how about this? You let me know if you get a media call, and I'll run it up the flagpole. If the boss says it's okay, you can do the interview. If not, our PR guy will take care of it."

"That's not an answer," Simon said, relaxing deep in Pilate's brain like the genie in his lamp.

"It's academic anyway, until January," the dean said, fanning his stubby fingers. "Looks like you get to fall into winter away from campus."

Pilate stood and extended his hand. "Sounds fine. I think the media's done with me for the most part anyway. They've moved on to real celebrities."

"*And you have a book to write,*" Simon goaded.

"Glad to hear it. I mean…" he held up his hand again, as if trying to stop the onset of any offense lured by his words.

"I understand," Pilate said. "See you in January."

"Great, John. That will be great." Felix turned away, absently biting his fingernail.

Pilate took one last glance at the office his dead friend once imbued with such cantankerous dignity, now occupied by a hapless interloper. Pilate hated Dean Felix, and that detesting wasn't really fair, as Felix's only crime was taking Trevathan's place.

His eyes fell to the floor as he gently pulled the door closed behind him.

Chapter Four

"Constable? What's that? Like…a dog catcher?" Pilate said, holding a gallon of milk.

County Commissioner Jeremy Ryder leaned against his white, late-model Dodge Ram at the convenience store on the edge of town. The pump clicked as he filled the thirsty tank. Laconic and reedy, Ryder took in the world with pale blue screw-you eyes and close-cropped, thinning, gray hair under his hat. He reminded Pilate of the post-millennium version of actor Peter Weller--no longer Robocop or Buckaroo Bonzai; rather, it was reminiscent of someone harder, reedier, and less tolerant of and patient about all the day-to-day bullshit. "Peace officer," he said, spitting tobacco juice on the ground near his ostrich boot; not a drop touched the leather.

"So…a cop?" Pilate squinted at the sunset behind Ryder.

"Not exactly," he answered, knocking the cowboy hat back on his head. "In this county, the sheriff is the number-one law enforcement officer, followed by the undersheriff and deputies."

"We don't have a sheriff," Pilate said. The last sheriff was shot in the throat and would never again eat solid food, let alone manage county law enforcement.

"As you well know, we also don't have an undersheriff," Ryder retorted. "Welliver didn't hire anyone for that job. He was so new after Scovill got put away. Scovill never hired an undersheriff, despite my strong suggestion to do so. He had Lenny for a deputy, but poor ol' Lenny's gone pretty much off the deep end into a bottle of hooch."

"What about the reserve deputies?"

"We've got a couple, and maybe one of 'em will run for sheriff." Ryder spat again. "That's another story. But for now, that's just two fellas handlin' law for the entire county. Hell, if it weren't for the state police and the local PDs, we'd be in some palpable discomfort."

"So..." Pilate said, the milk jug sweating in his hands. "What defines a constable's duties?"

"Jurisdiction. Sheriff's office protects a whole county, and the sheriff's deputies have the jurisdiction to prosecute crime in the county. Constables, under state law, are limited to townships too small for a police force." Ryder's eyes tracked two Cross College coeds who were crossing the parking lot with a pizza; he tipped his hat as they sashayed by.

"How come I've never heard of a constable in Cross?"

"Because the late, great Mayor Ollie Olafson, who you knew in most unfortunate circumstances," he said, wiggling his gray eyebrows up and down twice for emphasis, "named himself mayor and constable so he could pocket the enviable salary of $1,013 a month."

"Wow."

"Plus mileage." His eyes twinkled as he looked briefly at Pilate, then surveyed the pasture to the north, just across the road. Pilate knew the pasture well, having once walked it in a blizzard.

"That legal?"

Ryder shrugged. "Nope, but the county looked the other way. Was before my election to the commission. They had bigger fish to fry. Double O kept the peace, and that was that."

The gas pump continued clicking, doling out gallons for dollars.

"John, people around here are pretty evenly split about you," Ryder said, still eyeing the pasture. "They either love ya or hate your guts. I guess I'm a little more on the love-ya side of things, if you get my meaning."

"Gee, thanks."

"Maybe love isn't the right word." He cleared his throat and turned back to Pilate. "What I mean is, people respect you, one way or another, and you'd be a good choice to keep things orderly till we get a proper sheriff installed. Election's in a few weeks. All you gotta do is fly the flag, ya know?" He crossed his arms. "Make sure folks in Cross Township know somebody's paying attention."

"I'm not trained. I-I don't know anything about the law."

"You can read, can't you? You can shoot, and--"

"I'm not carrying a gun, Commissioner," Pilate said.

Ryder shrugged again, and his narrow shoulders danced under his Western-style shirt. "That's your business. You really don't need one anyway. You just carry a badge, serve the occasional subpoena, break up disturbances if necessary. As constable, you'll be tasked with keeping the peace, not pursuing hardened criminals or playing CSI. Traffic tickets, misdemeanors, minor felonies, college kids partying too hardy--that sorta thing."

The gas pump thumped to a stop, and the handle clicked back with a *thunk* as the Ram finished drinking.

Ryder removed the nozzle and jammed it back on the pump. "Things get hairy, you call the State Highway Patrol or the reserve deputies…or me."

"This county is 512 square miles," Pilate said, a fact he'd learned while writing his book, "and Cross is far from the county seat. Hell, the only reason the last two sheriffs were even around was because they both lived nearby. The reserve deputies live in the far side of the county, out in the sticks."

"And this isn't the sticks?" Simon snickered.

"State Patrol cruises Highway 75 twice a day," Ryder said, smiling. "Jesus, John, what are you worried about? You practically cleaned up the town singlehandedly already. There ain't any serious criminals to worry about. State folks will deal with drugs and heavy stuff."

"Like Hilmer Thurman?"

"Exactly. As constable, Thurman ain't your problem. Just let him be, and report any suspicious goings-on to Trooper Hulsey or that lieutenant what's-his-name at the state police…and me." Ryder replaced the gas cap with three *clicks*, then opened the door to his truck. "John, you don't gotta do anything but show yourself around Cross with a badge pinned on your shirt. Your call on weapons. The job's temporary, goes away at the discretion of the new sheriff, far as I'm concerned--assuming we can get somebody to run."

"Really? Nobody wants it?"

"With one former sheriff in the federal pen and the other eating his Big Macs through a tube? Ain't exactly a popular career choice 'round here."

"Gee, that just makes me want the job even more," Pilate said, shifting the gallon of milk to his left hand, wiping the condensation on his jeans.

"That's not the job you're up for," Ryder said, climbing in and closing the door. He rolled down the window. "You'd be Constable Pilate, issuer of parking tickets, enforcer of leash laws and scold to folks screwing in the park."

"Can I take some time to think about it?"

"Sure, John," Ryder said, firing up the Ram engine. "Meet me downtown tomorrow, at one."

"Where?"

"Constable's office, 'course," he said.

"I've lived here for a while now, and I didn't know there was constable, let alone an office," Pilate said.

"Ollie used it as his mayoral seat of power." Ryder's eyes shot up to his hat. "It's right next to the bank, funny enough."

"Might as well, John," Simon said. *"You could use $1,013 a month right now. Hell, who couldn't?"*

Plus mileage.

"See you there and then, Commissioner."

Ryder winked, smirked for an entire half-second, and slipped on mirrored aviator sunglasses. He made a clicking sound with his tongue and put the Ram in gear. He sped off with a wave of his index fingers on the steering wheel.

* * *

Pilate poked rather violently at the keyboard of his iMac. In two hours, he had managed to type:

BOOK PROPOSAL

Fighting Ghosts

The True Story of the End of the Cross College Conspiracy

by John Pilate

"That's it?" Simon mocked. *"And that title stinks."*

I got nothing else.

He planned to write about the events that took place after his first book, to cover what happened in Key West--of course leaving out the parts he swore to the Feds he wouldn't reveal on penalty of prison time. He would cover what happened when the former Cross College president snapped, his sociopathic nature blooming into full-blown psychopathy.

Pilate would detail nearly losing his wife, his unborn son, and stepdaughter. He was going to exorcise the demons, tell the tale of fighting off the ghosts from his past, and perhaps finally admit the truth about the ghost in his head.

"Are you an idiot?" Simon asked. *"You're gonna write a book telling the world that you have ghosts in your head? Do you want people's opinions of you to switch from a snarky, heroic everyman to a guy who needs to be admitted for observation and Thorazine cocktails?"*

Pilate didn't answer. He stared at the screen, the blinking cursor, the never-ending pulse of his writer's block. He leaned back in a small attic study he shared with numerous boxes of dusty crap. It was mostly stuff he moved in when he married Kate, but there were a few boxes of stuff that belonged to Kate's first husband, Richard. The man Pilate killed, Ollie Olafson, murdered him.

"Are you as tired as I am of all this incestuous small-town murder shit?"

Yes, Simon. Of course I am.

"Then maybe you should write a children's book. The Adventures of a Deranged Boy and His Imaginary Friend."

"Hmm…" Pilate deleted the words and typed:

BOOK PROPOSAL

Fighting Ghosts: A Novel

by John Pilate

"See, Simon?"

"Oh, I see. So now you just write it up like a novel, a little…creative nonfiction nicely disguised, eh?" he said. *"You leave the readers wondering how much of this is based on the truth and how much is fantasy?"*

"Exactly."

"I like it. You can even work in some exciting bits from your work as the town dog catcher. Get to work now, penman. Simon needs new pair of shoes."

Chapter Five

Kate Nathaniel Pilate munched contentedly on her salad, her eyes shining with just a hint of fatigue lingering at the corners.

"Dorothy Lynch?" Pilate asked, looking at her salad then around the Cross College cafeteria as it started to empty.

She nodded, chewing greens doused in the sweet and spicy, thick and creamy salad dressing.

"I tried. Still like ranch better."

"Meh, it's a Nebraska thing." She speared more salad with her fork.

"Gee. Are you starving or what?"

"Yeah…and I don't know why," she said, her blonde hair falling around her eyes. She brushed it back. "Just been ravenous lately."

"Uh-oh," he said.

"Oh, stop."

"You're right, he smiled. "Except for one historically exceptional case, pregnancy requires sexual activity."

Kate gave him the facial version of the finger and continued to eat.

"Sorry."

"It's okay," she said, sipping ice tea. "Having kids isn't much of an aphrodisiac, is it?"

"No, not at all," Simon said. *"Master Peter Pilate's crying shrinks me member like a spider on a hot stove."*

"It's okay, babe," Pilate said. "It's probably more about me being a miserable bastard because of Frechette." Pilate nodded at a student who walked by, staring at him and Kate. He was still a celebrity to some on campus, especially the kids.

"They'll catch 'im," she said, dabbing her mouth with a napkin. "They'll get your money back too. Besides, even if they don't, I know your next book will kick ass."

"And in the meantime?"

"In the meantime, we're fine. My salary plus the money from the sale of the funeral home--"

"That's Kara's inheritance, not a mortgage payment."

"Well, even our well-educated Kara will be on the street right there with us if we don't pay the mortgage, and we need that money to pay it." Kate bit into her sandwich.

"How much is the mortgage?"

Kate swallowed, then bit her lower lip. "Nine eighty-five a month."

"Well, what if I could come up with some cash to help pay for that?"

"That'd be great," she said. "Bummer there's no teaching sections for you till next semester. Maybe if Monique gets you a magazine story--"

"Or…I could be the town constable."

She stopped chewing. "What?"

"Commissioner Ryder asked me yesterday."

"Jeremy Ryder? Whoa. The man, the myth, the legend? When did you see him?"

"Last night, when I went to get milk. He was filling up his Ram."

"And you're just telling me now?"

"Sorry. Peter's colicky, and you were--"

"Ryder's a real piece of work. Been around for ages. Hmm." She paused a moment, looking off into space, as if recalling something from long ago.

"What? You know him?"

"Not exactly. He's got quite a history. I think he was a big hero, an Army Ranger or something, and then he was sheriff a couple counties over." Her face changed back to normal in an instant. "Constable? Really? We haven't had one of those in this town since…well, ever," she said, swallowing, then chuckling. "I mean, Ollie used to pin that badge on for every Founders' Day or OakFest, but Scovill was the law, such as it was."

"I know, and it's not really a big deal--just parking tickets and stuff. Still, it'd cover the mortgage."

"You're serious, aren't you?"

"I'm meeting him downtown in twenty minutes."

"John, you need to spend your time writing and--"

"It's a safe gig, hon'," he said. "It pays about a grand a month, plus mileage...and it'd get me outta the house."

"Or," she said, picking up her sandwich, "it could be dangerous."

"More dangerous than getting shot by the former mayor or fighting off the pirates of the Caribbean? C'mon! It's nothing, really. I won't even need to carry a gun."

"No weapon?" Her forehead wrinkled. "John, you know I have almost zero love for guns, but they've saved our lives several times over the past two years. If you're gonna do this, maybe you should carry one."

"I'll think about it," he leaned back in his chair, stretching. "Maybe I'll just carry a bullet in my pocket."

She smirked and looked at her watch. "I have to get to class. Let's talk about this at dinner, okay?" She scooted back her chair and stood.

These days, she wasn't wearing the painted-on Levi's she wore the first time he saw her; pregnancy seemed to decrease that possibility. Still, she looked radiant. Most of the baby weight was gone, though her face was a bit softer. His stomach fluttered a bit when she looked him in the eyes.

"Only growling because you didn't touch your lunch," Simon teased.

Pilate rose from his chair, leaned over the table, and kissed Kate's cheek. "Okay babe. Over dinner."

* * *

"As of the last census, there are 7,576 people, 3,047 households, and 1,980 families residing in our fair county," Ryder said, his pointy ostrich boots resting on the former mayor's (and constable's) huge, dusty oak desk. He gestured at a map of the county behind him. "Good news is, most of 'em are not your problem. Your concern is Cross Township." He pointed at a tiny area in the southeast portion of the county, outlined in red. "It's under the law enforcement jurisdiction of the town constable. That means you are the law when it comes to 865 people, 225 households, and 99 families. Add an extra 1,000 and change of mischievous students in fall and spring semester."

"I see," Pilate said, rubbing his chin, his stomach fluttering again, unpleasantly this time. "And who do I answer to? Besides the vacancy in the sheriff's office, there's no mayor until November either."

"Well, there's the town council--six of the least interesting, most fractious, tedious people you'll ever meet. The chairman…er, chairperson is Calista Thorson. She's acting mayor. Sixty-eight years old and more worried about her sewing club getting free iced tea at the diner than she cares about actually running the town," Ryder said, shifting his right boot under his left on the desk. "Just tip your hat when they come 'round, and be earnest and perfunctory when you go to council meetings."

"I can do earnest and perfunctory."

"Yup, I figured you could." He pointed his finger at Pilate like a gun and clicked his tongue. "So, beyond the civilities you afford the council, you just answer to me."

"Okay," Pilate said, scanning the small office for remnants of the possessions of his former nemesis, Ollie Olafson: most noticeably the dust on the desk and shelves, an unused copy of the Yellow Pages, and three National Rifle Association member stickers peeling from the window glass. A empty gun rack hung, forlorn, by the door, as if grieving its former owner's demise. Pilate noticed also that the large storefront windows and door had heavy wooden shutters on the inside that could swing open to let the light in or be locked shut, presumably for security reasons.

"Does that mean you're in?" Ryder said, eyebrows raised.

Pilate nodded. "Let's see how it goes."

"That's the spirit," Ryder answered gleefully, then flipped something small and shiny on the desk.

"What's that?"

Ryder stood and pulled his Wranglers up by his large bronze belt buckle. "A little tarnished, but it's serviceable."

Pilate picked up a seven-pointed brass badge with the words "CONSTABLE" and "CROSS TOWNSHIP" imprinted in the center.

Ryder handed Pilate a heavy black plastic box.

"And what's this?"

"Your sidearm," he said. "It's a .38. I know you know how to use it."

"I'll wear the badge, but I don't want the gun."

"Ya never know what you'll run into out there," Ryder said, contradicting his own nonchalance and grinning with tobacco-yellowed teeth.

"I've had enough of guns, Commissioner."

"Kidding, John. I get it." He waved Pilate's indignation off. "Keep it in your desk if you want, but I have to issue it to you. I'll get you a permit. There's also a varmint gun—a shotgun with birdshot--to take care of rabid dogs, skunks, Democrats, etc. It's locked in the jail cell."

"Jail cell?"

"Yep." Ryder's eyes smiled in the shade of his hat brim. "C'mon. She's back here."

Pilate followed Ryder through a side door that led past a toilet, into a small back room with an eight-by-ten jail cell. Encased in blue steel bars, it contained a cot with a blanket and a sweat-stained pillow. The jail area also doubled as a small break room, as it was equipped with a microwave, mini-fridge, and a flimsy card table that looked as if it might not be able to support the weight of a full deck or a bowl of ramen.

Ryder produced a key and opened the cell door. "I'd say 1897 or so." He pulled back the blanket on the cot, revealing an old shotgun. "Shells are in the desk. I'd carry it in my car, if I were you--in case of varmints and such."

"And such, huh?"

"You need a gun rack?"

"In a Saab?"

Ryder regarded him for a moment. "A Saab?" He looked like he was going to spit on the floor. "What happened to that Batmobile of yours, that black Grand Am or whatever the hell it was?"

"I was driving the Saab the other night," Pilate said, recalling their meeting at the gas station.

"Shit, I thought that was your wife's car," Ryder said. "No offense."

"Why should you take offense?" Simon said. *"Oh. Wait. Because you're driving a girlie car!"*

"The Pontiac was never the same after Ollie ran me off the road--you know, before all that mess got into high gear. Besides, I kinda like the old Saabs," Pilate said of the 2001 9-3. "They have character. Found one in St. Joe, only 63,000 miles on her. Mechanic says she could easily go another 100,000--"

"Okay. Whatever, ya Swede. At least it's not a convertible. It's probably the only one in the county, so you'll stand out for sure. Put the shotgun in the trunk. Those chick buggies do have trunks, right?" Ryder handed Pilate the keys to the jail cell and the office. "Probably in the front or something," he muttered.

Pilate accepted the keys.

"You'll note there's a back door that leads to the alley. Used to transport prisoners out that way, back in the old days, to avoid the screaming mobs out front." He snorted. "Handcuffs, ticket book, rules and regs, and county bylaws also in the desk. Paperwork's in the center drawer for you to fill out and sign. Get it over to me Monday so I can get you on the payroll."

Pilate nodded. "Is there a broom or something so I can clean this dump up?"

"In back. Sorry there's no trusty to do it for ya, unless maybe you arrest somebody and sentence them to hard labor." Ryder chuckled.

"Uh-huh."

"Well, I set up an orientation for you with Trooper Hulsey, of the state police. He's gonna come by my office Monday at ten, so be there. We'll give you a crash course in Constable 101, Professor."

"Okay, Commissioner," Pilate said. "Thanks."

Ryder offered his hand, and Pilate took it.

"Well, I'll shake your hand, but I was asking for the badge," he said.

"Why?"

"So I can pin it on you, dumb butt."

Chapter Six

"This is so embarrassing," Pilate said.

"It is not," Kate said, rubbing the constable badge with brass cleaner. "Can't have my sexy constable walking around with a tarnished badge." She rubbed it furiously a moment, eyed it, and pulled him to her so she could pin it on his shirt. "There."

"'Sexy' and 'constable' don't seem like words that go together," Simon mocked.

"Honey, do I have to wear it?"

"Absolutely, especially on your first day. Go make your rounds, meet the people, and--"

"Everybody knows everybody in this microscopic burg, so--"

"Yes, but now you'll meet and greet them as Pilate the Peace Officer, not Pilate the Prick." She laughed.

"Kiss my ass," he said.

"You wish. Now get out there and do your damn job," she said. "Do you have your card with the Miranda warning printed on it?"

"Yes, but I'm really not supposed to arrest--"

"Do you have your citation book?"

"In the car," he said.

"This really is embarrassing," Simon said.

"Do you have your town bylaws and codes manual? The sash with your merit badges?"

He kissed her. "Brat. See you later."

"Wait! I made you a sack lunch with a chocolate pudding cup."

* * *

"I've had enough of you," he said, his tone even, as if he had strenuously rehearsed the five words. "I want you outta my life. You're not good for me or my family."

"Keep going, John."

"You're not necessary. You make things more complicated. I have a wife and family now. You're superfluous. You're all the complications of a…of a…"

"An affair, John?" Simon hissed. *"Is that what you were going to say? I'm all the complications of an affair but none of the fun?"*

"I can't do this anymore, Doc," Pilate said, staring at the speakerphone on his constable desk.

"You can, John. Keep going," Sandburg coaxed, his tinny voice issuing from the small speaker. "This is good."

"You're killing me, John, and I don't deserve a death sentence for sticking with you all this time," Simon said--his voice far from tinny.

"Doc, is this really necessary? I mean, Simon's not hurting me. Really, he just--"

"Simon?" Sandberg cleared his throat. "Excuse me, John, but this Simon is not a 'he'. It is a prop, a vestige of false support. You don't need it anymore. It's time you cut it loose. This is for the best, John."

"You said he'd go once I got back on my medications," Pilate interrupted. "I take 300 milligrams of Wellbutrin a day, and he's still here. He's just…quieter is all."

"Send somebody," Simon said. *"I need help."*

"This feels wrong," Pilate said, rubbing his eyes. "I'm killing him, and he's like…a friend."

"That's right," Simon said.

"Kind of a bastard, but a friend all the same."

Simon sighed.

"John, you're clinging to this figment of your imagination, and it's getting in the way of your thought processes and complicating your life. You came to me about this, and I made a special arrangement to work with you by phone--"

"How is Key West anyway? Storms blow over?"

Pilate heard Sandberg drop something on the desk, his glasses or perhaps a pen; the doctor was obviously frustrated about the abrupt change in subject. "John, I get paid whether we talk about the weather or your neuroses. If you don't want to do this, let's call it done, and you and Simon can get on with being the man with two brains."

"Damn, Doc, you sound stressed," Pilate said.

"Maybe he should find someone to talk to about all that pent-up tension," Simon agreed.

"I just don't want to indulge in wasting time when we're trying to get you healthy, especially now that you have a potentially stressful new job."

"What ever happened to letting a patient work through things at his own pace?"

"John, perhaps you're right. What does Simon say?"

"How about nothing?" Simon said.

"Nothing," Pilate said.

Sandberg cleared his throat again. "Okay, John. You have fifteen minutes left in this session. What do you want to talk about?"

"I guess we could discuss about how angry I am about losing everything."

"Money isn't *everything.*"

"Proof yet again that the good doctor is and always will be full of shit. How much is he charging you per hour?" Simon said.

"Well, it's everything if it means I'm stuck in Cross Township, writing parking tickets till I get a whole lot more of it."

"Hmm. Well, let's say you get your money back. Where will you go?"

"I don't know, Doc. Away."

"You'll run away again?"

"To sanity, perhaps," Pilate countered.

"Fair enough. I won't deny that, as your doctor, I'd like to see you living somewhere less fraught with bad memories, but for the time being, you have some good medicine to make it bearable."

"I already told you that the medication doesn't help much."

"I meant Kara, Peter, and Kate."

"Oh." Pilate breathed deeply, exhaling directly into the speaker.

"Are you smoking?"

"No. If it does nothing else, the Wellbutrin is great for helping a man obey the surgeon general's warnings. I gotta give it that. Just needed a...what's the psychobabble for it? Cleansing breath?"

"Maybe you can elaborate on the need for the cleansing breath."

"No," Pilate said.

"Tell him, John," Simon whispered.

"Maybe..." He stopped himself. "Well, maybe I just feel overwhelmed."

"By fatherhood?"

"By everything--fatherhood, marriage, career, life, death..."

"Welcome to midlife," Sandberg chuckled.

"I'm only forty."

"Well, welcome to full-blown adulthood then," he retorted. "Take your pick."

"It's like I boarded Space Mountain alone, had a wild ride, and arrived at the end with a wife, kids, money problems, and--"

"Don't forget your imaginary pal!" Simon said.

"John, you're not going through anything unusual. Every self-aware person goes through this sort of thing. I will give you this. Most of them aren't surviving murder attempts and being stalked by psychopaths who bugged their psychiatrist's office."

"Yeah. Sorry about that whole bugging thing."

"Not your fault."

"I just never feel at peace."

"Never? John, do me a favor. Breathe deeply again. Blow it out. Think for a second. Have you *ever* felt at peace? Don't answer right away. Think about it. If you have, where and when was it?"

Pilate inhaled, held the breath deep in his lungs, then let it go. "On the *TenFortyEZ*, last time Taters and I went fishing. We just drank Modelo, shot the shit and fished. Hell, we really didn't talk much, but it was such a carefree, peaceful time."

"So your refuge is an aging fishing charter, in the waters off Key West, in the company of a buddy?"

"Yeah, I guess so. That's bad, right?"

"Why would it be bad?" Sandberg asked.

"Because it seems to indicate that I view my family as a chore, or at least something that isn't all that peaceful. That can't be good, so it's gotta be bad."

Sandberg laughed. "Oh, John, I'm pretty sure if we asked Kate the same question about being at peace, you and the kids wouldn't be in the picture. In your family, you play the role of protector, breadwinner, etc. With your friends, your only job is to be your true self. That's a lot easier when you're drinking a cold one, bobbing up and down on the water, basking in the sun."

"I guess I've never thought of it that way," he said.

"Does Simon ever horn in on your time with Taters Malley on the boat?"

Pilate cast his mind back. "You know, now that I think about it, not too much."

"Who can get a word in edgewise with that Jimmy Buffett-wannabe-fish-smelling redneck?" Simon said.

"Would it be fair to say that Simon is heard most when you're stressed or unsure of yourself?" Sandberg said.

"Piss off," Simon said.

Pilate sat up in his chair. "Crap, Doc. You're right."

"Then you *do* need to work on getting him out of your life. He's not an effective coping mechanism for stress or fear," Sandberg admonished.

"But I'm a whole helluva lotta fun at parties."

"I don't know how to do that," Pilate said.

"Thus, the need to stop now and schedule our next session."

* * *

"I've had just about enough of you," Pilate said. "You need to go. You're causing a disturbance, upsetting the other guests."

"That's not true, Sheriff," the man slurred, his breath toxic and fermented.

"Constable."

"What?"

"Constable, not sheriff, but close enough."

"I don't see no gun or uniform--just a tacky dime-store badge. My kid got one of them damn things outta a bubblegum machine. Did yers cost a whole quarter?"

"No, I don't have a gun, but if you want me to get someone with a gun over here, I can make a call to the state police. They tend to listen to those of us wearing dime-store badges a whole lot more than they're gonna listen to a ridiculous drunk."

The drunken man cast a bleary gaze at Pilate and Cusack, the bed-and-breakfast owner. He shrugged and looked at the mortified woman beside him, presumably his wife.

"Come on. Up with you," Pilate said. "Cusack's agreed to waive your bar bill if you move along. Now get up and let your wife take you to your room."

The portly tourist rose unsteadily, knocking the small table with his knee. "Sorry state of affairs when a man's forced out of a public house by fuckin' Barney Fife."

"Like I said, I can call Andy Taylor, or maybe even John T. Chance if you'd like," Pilate said.

The drunk waved him off, leaning on his crimson-faced wife.

"Sorry, Sheriff," the humiliated missus mouthed.

"Constable," Pilate mouthed, smiling as the two tottered upstairs.

"Mr. Pilate, you did a fine job there," Cusack said, smiling. "We don't get many like that, and I can usually handle 'em, but this one was a wee bit argumentative. Marcy got worried I'd hit the fella."

Pilate laughed.

"Tell the truth and shame the devil," Cusack said. "Stay for a drink?" His eyes smiled, as if he knew an amusing secret.

Pilate shrugged. "Why not? I'm off duty anyway." Pilate pulled up a seat at the bar in the cozy pub of the Cross and Cork Inn.

"What's your poison, Constable?" Cusack said, wiping his hands on a bar towel and picking up a glass.

"Vodka."

Cusack made a face. "Sorry. I thought you wanted a drink, not a glassful of paint thinner."

"Of course. Silly me. I'll have two fingers of Cork's finest."

Cusack gave an approving look as he pressed the glass to the optic dispenser of Jameson's. "Our James'll take the chill outta ya."

"It's not that chilly."

"Then it will put one in ya," Cusack said. "Oh, where are my manners? Rude to make you drink alone." He filled his own glass. Cusack's accent could be a trial to understand at times, but the Jameson's helped.

"Where's your better half?"

"Doin' her thing upstairs. It's late, and we don't have but two rooms filled tonight."

Pilate took a gulp. Though he was not especially partial to whiskey, he decided it was something he could get used to.

Cusack and Marcy had moved to the county a year ago and purchased the thirty-room Carlson mansion, a structure built in 1866 by the Carlson family, on the edge of downtown Cross. The Carlson family had settled much of the area between Cross Township and what was now known as Goss City, and they'd made their fortune moving freight up and down the Missouri by steamboat. Pilate remembered the late Derek Krall, Cross Township's de facto historian, saying the Carlsons had cleaned up even more during the Civil War by "picking the right side."

The mansion was occupied until the flood of 1943, which rerouted the course of the Missouri and flooded the stately old pile. The Carlsons went bankrupt trying to restore the property to its former glory, and most of them moved away into obscurity or died off. It was empty in 1963, when just a few blocks away, Professor Brady Bernard killed Cross College President Walker Keillor and Dean Gareth Kennedy, then himself.

By the late sixties, a string of new buyers had purchased the mansion and made a go of it as a B&B. The Cusacks were the latest owners, and they'd named it quite appropriately. Cusack and Marcy refurbished the old manse in the style of an Irish pub and bed-and-breakfast, and the Cross and Cork quickly became one of the most popular B&B's in southeast Nebraska.

Cusack married Marcy, a Cross College grad, after they met at a pub in his hometown of Cork, when she and a friend visited Blarney Castle. He warned her off kissing the Blarney Stone. "If people only knew what the kids do to that stone at night," Cusack once told Pilate, shaking his head slowly.

The Cross and Cork did well, especially with tourists who visited for OakFest or journeyed in to watch the leaves change. It was close enough to the college that it filled up on homecoming and parent weekends too. Pilate enjoyed the little bar. It almost made him feel as if he'd been whisked away from Cross Township temporarily, though it did scare up a few daunting memories of his British ex-wife.

"How's the constable business? You been at it how long? A week?"

"Yeah." Pilate sipped the Jameson's, enjoying the warmth on his tongue. "It's boring, but at least the pay is shitty," he said, smiling into his glass.

"Wife and kids?"

Pilate liked that about Cusack. Whenever the man talked to anyone, he genuinely appeared interested in what they had to say and how they actually were doing. "They still tolerate me," Pilate said.

Cusack snatched up his glass. "Another?"

"No thanks. Driving…and I'd like my wife to continue tolerating me." Pilate dropped a ten on the bar.

Cusack turned his back to Pilate and raised a bushy silver eyebrow. "Somebody dropped a tenner on the bar. Is it yours?"

"Cusack, I'm a public official."

"Correction, buddy. You're an *off-duty* public official."

Pilate smiled and tucked the bill back in his pocket. "Thanks." He stood up, extending his hand.

Cusack turned back to Pilate and offered his hand as well, though his eyes looked past Pilate and landed on an older gentleman with a neatly trimmed mustache who walked in and took a seat at the end of the bar.

"Heya Dave," Cusack said. "Usual?"

The man nodded at Cusack and fished in his pockets for a cigar.

"See ya next time. Say hi to Marcy for me," Pilate said.

"What? Oh. Yeah, will do, buddy." Cusack smiled, turning his attention back to Pilate. "And hello to your boss too."

Pilate wanted another drink, truth be told, so when he got home, he had one, sitting in the back yard. With Colin Hay's "Me and My Imaginary Friend" played on the stereo and his butt planted in an Adirondack chair, Pilate contemplated book proposals and backyard bars.

Chapter Seven

Jackie the Crow downed a shot of Jameson's and polished it off with a swig of Budweiser. "Piss," he muttered, wiping his mouth on the sleeve of his denim jacket. He glanced around the smoky roadhouse, his head throbbing and his eyes watering. As he placed the Bud on the bar, he observed sparse white hairs that had sprouted from the gnarled knuckles on his left hand. He came by his misshapen digits honestly; he mused silently that the knuckles were the only honest characteristic he possessed.

"Another?" Nelda offered, moving her head slightly. as if trying to move her hair from her eyes, an impossible feat, considering that she'd used enough Aqua Net to keep Lornamead profitable.

Jackie eyed the rail-thin woman's apprehensive stance behind the bar. Her skin was deeply tanned, her bleach-blonde hair immovable, and her t-shirt far too young for her age.

He pointed at the shot glass. "This, not that."

"You that Scotch fella who owns the new B&B?"

The man looked at her blankly, cold and disinterested. Then he winked. "Irish…and no. You've got me confused with some other Mick."

Normally, Nelda would have pressed on and asked plenty of nosy, prying questions, making witless American conversation about how half her family was from Ireland or some such prattle, but something about Jackie the Crow's face told her he was best left alone. Instead of blabbing, she nodded, poured him a shot, and turned her attention to a cigarette that was smoldering in an ashtray behind her.

Jackie's fat knuckles moved for the shot glass, but he stopped. "Keep your wheels turnin'," he said. "I'm only foolin' with ya. Yeah, I know Cusack."

She brightened, cautiously inquisitive. "Well, why aren't you drinkin' at his place?"

"Too dear."

Nelda raised an eyebrow, uncomprehending.

"Can't afford his overpriced booze. 'Sides, he annoys me."

The door to the Brown Betty swung open, allowing light to pour in for a few seconds. Jackie glanced at the figure of the new patron in the mirror. The patron slipped a dollar in the jukebox and selected "Green, Green Grass of Home."

As the first few notes played, Jackie looked over his shoulder at the patron. "Speak of the Devil," he said to Nelda. "Annoyin' me again. Well, well, well," he said over the music. "Leave it to a half-Welsh, half-Mick to pick a tune by that tight-trousered tosser. What, 'Raglan Road' not good enough for ya"?

"Jackie," Cusack said, his face blank as he slid onto the beat-up leather barstool beside him.

"Cusack the Corkie," Jackie said.

Cusack signaled another round of Jameson's and beer. After Nelda slid them over, he sighed. "So…what brings you here?"

"I figured you'd already know that," Jackie said, then downed his shot.

"I left all that behind me, Jackie," Cusack said, his drinks untouched. "I thought we agreed that once I left Cork, we'd be even."

"I reckon that could be how you see it," Jackie said, looking at Cusack in the mirror hanging behind the bar, "but the way I see it, you still owe me, and I'm here to collect."

Cusack felt a wave rush over his features. He knew his face was growing ruddy and hot, as it always did when he wanted to mangle someone. "What do you want?"

Jackie the Crow smiled and cawed quietly under his breath, quite like his avian namesake.

"I'm not giving you my place," Cusack said adamantly, raising his voice, his face reddening.

"Didn't ask ya to."

Nelda, observing through the mirror a few feet away, thought Cusack looked like he wanted to pick up his beer bottle, smash it in the other Irishman's face, and drink the shot to celebrate.

"What then?"

"You got a good ting here, Cusack the Cork," Jackie said, smiling and speaking in an unnervingly precious voice, like a cartoon leprechaun. "I asked 'round. Folks tink you're just a sweet Irish guy, adding a wee bit o' color to this boring shithole, shilling the blarney for dumb, fat-arsed Americans, wearing a queer tam o'shanter and tellin' 'em stories about the pot o' gold and all that shite."

"I run a business that serves good, decent people," Cusack said quietly, looking at Jackie's reflection in the mirror.

"Right, and I want what's mine--my portion."

"I owe you nothing," Cusack said, his eyes burning under his bushy silver eyebrows.

Jackie's hand traveled under the lip of the bar and quickly grasped Cusack's balls in an unforgiving grip.

Cusack started and grabbed Jackie's arm. "What the…?"

"Easy, Corkie," Jackie said. "Just hear me out, and I'll let yer goolies go."

"Get on with it," Cusack said, his face a red, ripe strawberry.

Nelda crept closer to the end of the bar, her hands blindly grasping for a hidden panic button.

"Twenty-five grand, and I go away," he said. "That money crosses my palm, and the vice comes off your balls."

Cusack gasped. "Where the fook--"

Jackie squeezed, and Cusack checked his volume, taking it down a notch, just under Tom Jones.

"Where the fook do ya think I'm gonna get twenty-five? Or five, for that matter? I run a fookin' B&B, not a damn gold mine."

Jackie shrugged. "Don't know, don't care. My tourist visa lasts for several weeks yet, so I'll just check on you from time to time, 'til I get my due. Maybe you oughtta put off your real estate purchase plans."

"Ya damn fool! How do you think you'll move twenty-five kay out of the country?"

"Leave that to me, boyo," Jackie said, finally releasing Cusack's manhood. "Now, outta respect, I'll stay away from your place, but you best be here next Friday, same time, with the money or a good reason why you don't got it."

"And what if I my reason isn't good enough?" Cusack asked, fearing the answer.

"Well, let's not get into further unpleasantness at this juncture," Jackie said. He then nonchalantly downed Cusack's shot and lit a Marlboro.

Cusack turned to him, his face an inch from Jackie's, the veins in his temples throbbing. "You two-bit gangster. You tink you can come here, to my town--"

"*Your* town?" Instantly, Jackie's voice changed to what could only be described as an Irishman's inexpert approximation of an American accent, something like John Wayne crossed with James Cagney. "What, are you a true-blue 'merican citizen now?"

"You come riding in here like it's the old days and old places and think I'll just roll over? You fookin' bastard. You got no muscle. You got nothing but threats and bad fookin' breath. Get on with it and cause your trouble. You'll be sorry."

"I got no muscle, you say?"

"You heard me. You got nothin'." Cusack slid from his stool, turned on his heel, and strode to the door. He threw it open, letting the light of midday bathe the interior of the Brown Betty again.

Nelda nodded at Tom, who had taken in the last moment or two of the Irishmen's conversation from his table by the bar. He rose, hitched up his Rustler jeans, and went into his boss's office.

"Looks like that really got his attention," Tom said, smirking.

Hilmer Thurman smiled. "I'll bet, like Marley's Ghost showing up."

"Bob Marley, right?" Tom said, leaning against the wall in Thurman's tiny office.

"No," Thurman said, sipping black coffee from a chipped white mug. "Tell that little shit to get in here."

Chapter Eight

Town constables have the authority of arrest and to execute warrants, subpoenas, summons, and other court documents, but there certainly wasn't a lot of that sort of red tape going on in Cross Township. Pilate served one subpoena in his first week, earning a remarkable mileage reimbursement of $4.20.

Due to the lack of a sheriff, and by special dispensation from the county commission, Pilate was given complete law enforcement power within Cross Township city limits as well. He had most of the authority of a county sheriff, though he was told by Ryder to report anything beyond a civil nature--as in violence--to the state police to take action.

"That'll do you a helluva lotta good if you're caught in the crossfire at a robbery or handling a domestic violence case," Simon said. *"And why the hell aren't you carrying a gun? They said you can, as long as you get a permit, which they handed to you."*

"I'm done with guns," Pilate said aloud, his hands loose on the Saab steering wheel.

"You may live to regret that."

"Simon, shut up."

"Dr. Sandberg has turned you into quite the brute, you know."

Pilate told himself he was doing it as research, for his book.

"That's a laugh."

"Writing books is always a laugh," Pilate said. "I actually wrote a bestseller but didn't see one thin dime of the profits. Probably won't ever--"

"You're so boring when you're consumed with self-pity."

"Yeah, I guess I am."

"Now go check on that boy who won't stop crapping on Mrs. Drum's lawn."

* * *

Taters Malley used pliers to cut off the end of the fishhook stuck in the webbing of his right hand. He pulled the hook out of his throbbing paw, trying not to wince.

"Oh Mr. Malley, I am so sorry," the woman said, hopping up and down on the deck of the *TenFortyEZ* as if she were jumping an invisible rope, her breasts straining the blue bikini top in a way that made Taters forget his pain for a moment.

When he had reached for the hook in the Amberjack's mouth, it had jumped, causing Jean, the blue bikini-clad beauty, to shriek and jerk her pole up, pulling the line taut and burying the hook in Taters's hand. Shaking his head and swearing that he was fine, he cut the fish loose, then removed the hook. "It can happen to anybody," Taters said around the bloody hand in his mouth. "Just remember what I said about jerking the line like that."

"Yes, Jean, remember to be more careful," her companion said wryly. "Don't jerk it too hard now."

"Stuff it, Deb," Jean said, laughing.

Deb and Jean were in their mid-forties, both recently divorced, and in excellent shape, enjoying their first fishing expedition in the Gulf, courtesy of Taters's Tropical Tours. Back on the dock, they told Taters and his wife, Jordan, they'd dumped their husbands, who spent all their free time fishing. They wanted to see what was "so great about it." Taters had a suspicion that Jean and Deb were also a little closer than friends, but it wasn't his place to ask if they were fishing in each other's ponds.

Jordan shook her head slowly as Taters cast off and waved.

Three hours in, Taters spent fifteen minutes helping Jean wrestle a beautiful, sixty-pound greater amberjack, and they eventually hauled the thing aboard. Jean and Deb whooped in delight until the fishhook incident, exchanging their whoops for hopping on deck in mild panic.

Taters removed his hand from his mouth, smiled, and looked at his old Omega Seamaster watch, then the horizon. The sun was about an hour away from making its evening departure. Mallory Square was no doubt already filled with followers of the Green Flash. He let the amberjack tire itself out on the deck as the ladies continued their version of the pee-pee dance to avoid its thrashing.

"Well, ladies, we're approaching the moment in our cruise when we stop menacing the fish and have some refreshments before heading back to Key West."

"If we hurry, we can make the ghost tour," Deb said.

"Then let's go to that Hog's Snout Saloon," Jean said, making a soundless clapping gesture.

"Mr. Malley, is that a nice place?" Deb asked.

Taters looked pained for a second, then smiled. "Uh, yeah. Good conch fritters." He then leaned over the cooler, opened it, and felt the cool breath of the ice kiss his face. He scanned the Modelo, Bud, Kalik, and Shock Top bottles, mingling with token cans of Diet Coke and Sprite. "I've got beer, the best being Modelo, and--"

Suddenly, he felt something in his chest, as if someone had impaled him with a claw hammer. That was followed by the terrifying feeling of a balloon swelling with air under his sternum, with precious little room for expansion. He had been through such a thing before, only never so bad and certainly never while he was out on the Gulf. "Shit. Not again," he muttered. "Musta been that dance with the AJ."

"Mr. Taters, are you okay?" Deb said, her hands folded over her yellow bikini top in a gesture of concern.

Taters crumpled to his knees, then fell back heavily on his rump.

The pair of pretty brunettes examined his pale face with concern.

"Ladies, the good news is that you can have a beer. The bad news is that you'll have to open it and get that fish into the cold storage by yourselves."

Quizzical looks crossed their faces.

"Oh, and only after you make a call for me on the radio."

"What?" Jean said.

He pointed at the radio. "Pick that up. Right, Jean. You look like you can handle a radio just fine. Now push that button and repeat after me."

She clicked the handset.

"Good girl. Say, 'Mayday! Mayday! Mayday! This is the sailing vessel *TenFortyEZ*. This is the sailing vessel *TenFortyEZ*. This is the sailing vessel *TenFortyEZ*, declaring a medical emergency…'"

* * *

"Mrs. Drum, I spoke with Rocky, and he said Rocky Jr. has been disciplined," Pilate practically yelled in the elderly woman's ear.

Mrs. Drum's face looked as if she had French-kissed a lemon. "Sheriff, he has pooped on my lawn seven times. Seven!" The widow of a music professor--Dr. Drum, no less--Mrs. Drum was approaching eighty-five. However, she still possessed the energy of a sixty-year-old. She pointed at the large pile of fecal matter in the center of her otherwise immaculate front lawn.

"That kid must have eaten an entire can of corn," Simon said.

"Corn…er, I mean, constable," Pilate said, shaking his hand quickly.

"What?"

"Constable. I'm not a sheriff."

"Well, we had one till that creep Mostek shot him!" Her gaze flitted from the pile of crap to Pilate's badge. Poking the badge with a bony finger, she added, "Sheriff Welliver was a good man."

"Yes, yes, he was. I mean is. Is." Pilate reminded himself that Welliver was on permanent disability, not dead.

"And you caught the man. No, wait. You *killed* the man who shot him in the throat, didn't you?"

"Not exactly." He sighed. "It was actually another guy. He ran into a tree."

"What's that?"

"Ran into a tree, in an ambulance, at Monticello Cemetery. I hit him with a rented subcompact."

"Sounds a lot more heroic the way she tells it," Simon said.

"You should run for sheriff, John Pilate," the old one advised. "I saw you on *60 Minutes*." She then reeled her head back to the pile of human waste, stretching her wrinkly neck. "You get rid of that poop and make that little brat stop it, and I'll put a sign in my yard for ya."

"A sign?"

"'Vote John Pilate for Sheriff.'"

"Oh, no, I'm happy to help you with the poop situation, but I'm not running for sheriff."

"Why not? You're good with a gun," she barked, looking at his belt and adjusting her glasses. "Say, where's your hog leg?"

"Don't need it for hazardous waste incidents."

"What's that?"

"Corn!"

Chapter Nine

Hilmer Thurman walked through the foyer of Cusack's, nodding pleasantly at passersby. He loped into the pub area and eased into a seat at the bar, smiling as Marcy greeted him.

"What would you like, sir?"

Thurman shrugged. "Well, I tell ya, I hear this is an Irishman's place, so I figure I better have an Irish drink."

"Pish-posh," Marcy said; she watched a lot of *Masterpiece Theatre.* "You can have whatever you'd like."

Thurman smiled and shrugged again. "Whiskey it is then. Irish whiskey...neat."

Marcy smiled. "Comin' right up."

Thurman glanced around. No one else was seated at the small bar, but the four-tops were occupied by quiet drinkers. They seemed to be nice people, not the rowdy sort that typically patronized his Brown Betty Roadhouse. Thurman decided Cusack had a sizable crowd for a Friday night in the big town. *No wonder he's got money to burn on property speculation.*

"Lot of folks," Thurman said, accepting his drink.

Marcy surveyed the room. "Yeah, we're just about full up for OakFest."

An arboretum campus, Cross College hosted the OakFest every fall. The gathering featured family fun, sightseeing, lectures, and a craft show with items made of acorns and leaves. Thurman noted that not many of the festival-goers were likely to stop in at the Betty.

"Nice," Thurman said, sipping. "I was wondering."

"You're not here for OakFest?"

"No," he said. "I wouldn't know an oak from a maple." He laughed. "But I'm a townie."

"I thought there were no strangers left 'round here, since we got here six months back. I don't believe we've met though," she said. "I'm Marcy Cusack."

"Hil--"

Cusack, who barreled in behind the bar and past Marcy with a bucket of ice, cut him off. He slammed it into the bin and looked up at his wife. "There, my duck."

"Thanks, sweetie," Marcy said. "We need it. I was just chatting with this gentleman about how busy we are, full of OakFest fans."

Cusack turned, and his face fell at the sight of the local crime boss. "I see," Cusack said. "You've got him well taken care of with the Jameson's." He smiled. "Luv, would you mind checking the dryer? Need some fresh linens in the Dylan Thomas room, and maybe turn down The Elders on the stereo? It's a wee bit loud."

Marcy nodded, ran a hand through her crimson mane, and smiled at Thurman on her way to the back. "Come stay with us sometime… and bring the wife."

"Great idea," Thurman said, rising slightly in his seat to note her departure. "Lovely lady."

Cusack scanned the bar, then looked at Thurman. "Thanks. And what can I do for you, Mr. Thurman?" he asked, though it sounded more like "Turman" when it squeezed through Cusack's lips.

"Well, seeing as how you recently visited my establishment, I thought it only right to visit yours," he said.

"Well, I had a little business with one of your customers. You're welcome to finish your drink in peace," Cusack said, stepping away.

"I'm also here for a little chat, Mr. Cusack."

"I believe we've chatted more than enough already," Cusack said, folding his meaty forearms across his chest.

"Oh, come now, Mr. Cusack. Let's be polite with one another."

Cusack nodded. "What do ya want to discuss?" He looked behind him, through the door, to make sure Marcy wasn't near.

"Your bid on Mostek's store."

"That again, Mr. Thurman?" Cusack narrowed his eyes. "Like I already told ya, if you wanna buy that property, all you've gotta do is outbid me. I offered more than a fair price. Just ask Mr. Nemec."

"I don't want to ask Mr. Nemec. See, I do the telling, not the asking, and I'm telling you this in plain American English so you'll understand. I don't want to outbid you. To do that would mean being more generous than you to the widow Mostek. That would cost me money, Mr. Cusack. Money I don't have any desire to spend right now."

Cusack shrugged. "And what makes you tink today's answer will be different than last week's?"

"Look, I can make it worth your while to cooperate," Thurman said, his voice calm and gentle as he took another sip of whiskey.

Cusack picked up a bar towel. "Oh?"

"Yes. I'm prepared to make a little problem of yours go away."

"Problem? What problem is that?"

"A $25,000 problem."

Cusack looked into Thurman's dead eyes, then nodded. "I see. So you met Jackie the Crow?"

"The Crow?" Thurman chuckled. "Well, I know of an Irish fella named Jackie, who came into my place saying he's got some pricy beef with you. Hmm. Or would that be corned beef and cabbage?"

Cusack laughed, albeit a forced chuckle. "Jackie is an old friend. He's also a scammer. Got nothing I want."

"Well, I'm just saying, if you withdraw your bid on Mostek's store, I can make sure he doesn't scam you. Matter fact, I can make sure your old friend doesn't pester you at all."

"Just stop right there, Mr. Thurman. Jackie and I… We have our differences, but I wouldn't wanna see Jackie end up like Perry Mostek."

"Like Perry?" Thurman's eyebrows rose, and his jaw clenched. "Just what's that mean?"

"Well, he's gone and all, ain't he?" Cusack said. "Mostek just disappeared, like Hoffa or sometin'."

Thurman laughed. "You oughtta be very careful with that colorful imagination of yours. Perry shot the sheriff and took off. It's simple as that."

"So you say," Cusack said. "So you say. Some say he's dead, but others say certain…forces took care of him after he made a hash of the John Pilate situation."

Thurman glanced around the bar. "Look, we're gonna be interrupted anytime now, either by your lovely wife or some oak tree fetishist. Let's cut the bullshit, okay, Paddy? Mostek's gone. His place is for sale, and I want it at list price. Play ball and withdraw your bid, I'll see to it this Jackie Crow guy is, um…deported. Then I'll leave you and your family alone."

"What? Leave my family alone?" Cusack's eyes widened. He leaned in. "You mean the way you left John Pilate's family alone?" Cusack asked, his face red with fury.

Thurman stood, knocked back the whiskey, and placed the shot glass upside down on the bar.

Reflexively, Cusack grasped the glass and started to drag it across the bar toward him.

Thurman clamped down on Cusack's hand, then squeezed it until the glass broke, sending shards painfully into the flesh of the Irish barkeep's hand.

Cusack flinched but did not cry out.

"You cut yourself. You should be more careful," Thurman said, releasing Cusack's bloody hand. He smiled and walked out into the night.

* * *

Rocking in Kate's bentwood rocker, Pilate held the warm, sleeping swaddle of blankets and baby to his chest. It was a feeling of contentment he scarcely felt anywhere else.

"Not even on a fishing boat in the Gulf?" Simon snarked.

As if on cue, the telephone rang.

Pilate flinched, hoping the blare of the ringer wouldn't wake baby Peter Pilate from his slumber. "Shh, shh," Pilate cooed to his son.

He heard Kate pick up the phone in the kitchen and make muffled greetings.

Pilate figured it was his folks, checking on a date when the Pilate family of southeast Nebraska could make the journey to the Pilate family of central Oklahoma. They'd been after him for weeks to get down there so they could see that baby; every time, Pilate bit his tongue, resisting the Simonized impulse to quip that the road worked both ways.

The truth was that Pilate just didn't feel like going home. Though Cross Township was alien and far from what he would describe as home, he felt his home state was also a place where his detachment had transformed to an illogical resentment.

Whether it was fair to say so or not, Pilate believed that place of his upbringing had rejected him; it was the deathbed of his career, a marriage, and, for a long while, his hope. It was his literal birthplace and the home of his family, which he loved somewhat more fondly from a distance, but it was also a tomb for so many things he'd tried to bury. It was also the birthplace of Simon, and John Pilate was now forking over $150 an hour to try and rid himself of the scourge that was his alter-ego.

Kate appeared in the doorway. "John, it's Jordan."

"Jordan?" For a moment, he blanked. "Jordan Malley?" She had never called before. Hell, she hardly ever spoke.

Kate nodded hurriedly. "It's Taters. He had a heart attack."

* * *

The five feet between the rocker and the wall-mounted phone in the kitchen was enough of a commute for Pilate to experience the emotions of shock, disbelief, and dread. Mere weeks earlier, he'd lost his friend and mentor Peter Trevathan, and Taters was the closest thing Pilate had left to a best friend. "No," he said, matter-of-factly and definitively, as if drawing a line in the sand and daring the universe to cross it.

He handed Peter to Kate and took the phone. "Jordan, is Taters okay? How bad is it?"

"John, he's all right, but..." Jordan's normal reserve of cool was running low, and her voice cracked as it trailed off.

"But what?"

"It's so scary, John. He's awake and responsive, and they say it was only a minor attack, a warning, but they're concerned about his heart."

"Concerned?"

"Yeah. There's somethin' not quite right about it."

"What? It's blocked, right? That's serious but fairly routine," Pilate said. "Surely they can fix that."

"Well...not exactly," she said, regaining her composure.

"What do you mean?"

Pilate heard a voice in the background, asking for the phone.

"John, it's me, man."

"Taters? What the hell?"

"I had a minor heart episode, that's all," he said, in a voice that sounded like a recording of a recording. "I'm okay."

"Where did it happen?"

"On the *TenFortyEZ*, out in the Gulf, not too terribly far from that Bigfoot sighting." Taters snickered about the secret he and Pilate had sworn they would never reveal, on penalty of imprisonment by the Feds. "Had two little fillies out there fishin'. We hauled in a massive AJ, and I felt a pain, a pretty nasty one in my chest, like somebody shoved the Goodyear blimp down there. I had one of the gals call in a mayday. Coasties came out, and I was in a comfy bed at Lower Keys Med Center within an hour. That was when the fun began--needles and pokes and tests and what have you."

"So you actually had a heart attack?" Pilate looked at Kate, who was holding Peter tightly, with a look of concern frozen on her face.

"Well, not exactly," Taters mumbled. "It was a… Honey, what did they say?"

Jordan said something unintelligible to Taters.

"They did a scan and found out I have an alien heart." Taters was silent for two seconds, then started laughing until he coughed, a cough reminiscent of the wheezing croops Pilate's late friend Peter Trevathan frequently exhibited in the months before lung cancer took his life.

"Alien heart?" Pilate asked.

"Okay, here's the deal. Some cardiologist came in, a fella named Petals."

Jordan corrected him.

"Patelas? Yeah that. So anyway, this fella Patelas tells me that in twenty-five years of practice, he's never seen a heart like mine."

"What the hell is that supposed to mean?" Pilate said, pacing.

"I have extra arteries and veins and stuff. It's called collateral circulation. See, I had a widowmaker goin' on. My main artery was 100 percent blocked for quite sometime. That was what killed that Russert fella on *Press the Face*."

"Good Lord," Pilate said.

"Anyway, the doc gave me some literature about it. Honey, hand me that… No, that, the one Patelas left. A kneecap? Huh? Oh. Okay, Patel. Just give me… Thanks." He sighed as if the muddled conversation had winded him like a marathon. "My glasses?" Taters cleared his throat. "Thanks. Okay, let's see what this says. 'The heart has the ability to create collateral circulation, new vessels that help to nourish the myocardium when a blockage or a heart attack creates inadequate blood flow.' There ya go. I've got extra veins and stuff, basically a work-around for my heart, like a built-in cardiovascular detour."

"Well, thank God for that," Pilate said.

"Yeah, I'd be a goner if it weren't for that alien blood flow. I was doing pretty well up till a couple weeks ago, when I started getting chest pains. I thought it was just gas, but apparently, it wasn't."

"The widowmaker?"

"No. That was the collateral vessel, the work-around." He lowered his voice. "It's getting blocked, and if it gets blocked 100 percent too, that's it. Pfft. *Kobayashi Maru*."

"So what now?"

"Well, the doc gave me some nitro pills and some Crestor and some other kinda high-priced prescription Drano to try and get rid of the blockage," he said. "They want me to try their little cocktail for a couple weeks, see if it does any good. I'm not in immediate danger, but I've got some decisions to make."

Pilate exhaled, feeling as if he'd been holding his breath for a full five minutes. "Okay. And what are these decisions?"

"Jordan, honey, could you get me a Modelo?"

"No."

Pilate couldn't make out all of Jordan's words, but that refusal came across loud and clear.

"Okay, fine. Juice will be great, long as it's cold. Yeah, that. At least it looks like beer." After a short scuffle, Taters spoke back into the phone. "John, you there?"

"Yep."

"Okay, she's outta the room. Here's the deal. They're putting me on the meds for two weeks. If the blockage on my alien vein don't clear up enough, they want to try and push a stent or two up there."

"Well, stents are pretty safe. Why not do that right away? Why wait?"

Taters cleared his throat. "Because of the way my heart is made... well, inserting a stent could rupture the extra vein. They'd have to have a cardiac team ready to crack my chest and do a bypass right then and there."

"Oh jeez," Pilate whispered, leaning against the doorjamb, his eyes looking into his back yard, though not focusing on anything in particular.

"I don't want my chest cracked."

"Who would?" Simon said.

"But that's a maybe, not a certainty, right?"

"Right, but the upshot is, it could easily kill me. That's the Taters Malley theory anyway."

"I understand. So what are you gonna do?"

"Well, I figure I'll get out of this bed tomorrow, do a charter this weekend..."

"You most certainly will not!" Jordan said, full-throated. "Here. Drink this."

"John? Jordan again."

"I figured."

"He needs to get some rest, get away from stress," she said.

"Okay. I'll call back later."

"That's not what I mean. He needs to get away from here, away from Key West and that godforsaken boat of his. As long as he's here, all he'll think about is trolling around that damn Gulf."

"Honey, please," Taters said.

"Okay, so what are you going to do?"

"I'm not really sure yet, but how much does it cost to ship a fisherman to you via UPS?"

Chapter Ten

Once Jordan assured him that with medication and a light schedule Taters would be in no danger traveling to the middle of America, Pilate enthusiastically embraced the notion. Taters complained about losing revenue and closing down his business for a few weeks, but his protests were as shallow as low tide.

"Well, at least now I can finally get a look at that crazy town you're always going on about," Taters said. "Besides, I miss your sweet Kate and your babies."

Jordan planned to send Taters along a couple days later. She would stay behind to close up the boat and office, then join them in a week or so. Until then, Taters would have the Pilate family guestroom to himself, along with all the peace and quiet a small town, a seven-year-old, and a practically newborn infant could offer.

"Taters, it'll be our pleasure to have you," Pilate said into the phone.

"Is the missus okay with this?"

Kate smiled and nodded enthusiastically.

"If she isn't, I don't know what she's grinning about. I assume that means she'll be happy to see you and have me out of her hair while we do guy stuff."

"Yep," she said, then took fussy Peter upstairs.

"John," Taters said, his voice serious and low, "I'm okay. Really, man."

"Shit, Taters, I know that. I just have one question."

"Shoot."

"Can you drink beer?"

"Do fish screw in the Gulf?"

"Cool. Well, call me when you get your flight all set."

"Okay, pal…and, John…"

"Yeah?"

"Please tell me you have an ocean somewhere near your house."

"We have a pond a few acres in, and there's a river. Nearest lake's an hour away. Nobody here has even seen an ocean, except on *Baywatch* or *Jaws*."

"Crap."

* * *

Pilate busied himself finishing up the Frontdoor Backyard Bar. He sunk six-by-sixes in Quikrete and made sure they were level, but he needed help hauling the heavy oak door up on top of the posts.

"Call Riley Pierson," Kate volunteered. Even if she was so inclined, she couldn't possibly participate in any hard manual labor, in light of her recent C-section.

"Pierson's in town?" After graduation, Riley had moved to Lincoln and taken a job at a financial planning firm.

"Yup," she said. "I saw his mom at the gas station. He's here for the weekend. Oh, and I've got some tiki lights in the attic. I'll get them out."

Riley Pierson arrived twenty minutes after Pilate called. Apparently, the bright lights of Lincoln had made Cross Township hopelessly boring, and any distractions were welcomed.

"Hey, Nebraska. What ya been up to?" Pilate asked.

"Did a little hunting with Dad," he said, rubbing his cheek.

"Oh yeah. That's right. You're a dead-eye shot, won the Nebraska State Shooting Contest or something, right? Isn't that why the guys call you 'Nebraska'?"

"Yeah, at first it was the Nebraska Kid, but Nebraska for short. But you wouldn't know it by the way I performed this morning," he said. "Didn't hit a damn thing."

"Everybody has an off day, right? How's Abbey?" Abbey and Riley had been Pilate's students, and, notwithstanding Abbey's longstanding crush on Pilate, the pair eventually started dating.

"She's good," Riley said, grunting as he helped Pilate lift the heavy door up onto the posts.

"Okay. Just hold that there while I screw in the brackets," Pilate said, ducking under the door with his electric screwdriver. Once it was horizontal, it looked like some semblance of a bar. "She's still teaching, right?"

"Uh-huh," Riley said. "Elementary school."

"And junior high in the same building, as I recall, but Abbey's teaching first grade?"

"Yup."

The screwdriver worked the screws into the old wood. The door squealed as if it was being stabbed; the screwdriver wheezed to sink the screws.

"So, how are you guys coping with you being an hour away?"

"Well, uh..." Riley said. "Screws goin' in?"

"Yep," Pilate said, "as good as can be expected."

"We're coping okay."

"Good. Please tell her hi from me."

"Huh? Don't you see her? I mean, with Kara going to school there and all and you being the new sheriff and all, I thought you might see her around town?"

"Not much," Pilate said, "Kara's in Mrs. Molloy's class, and it's constable."

"Huh?"

"Constable, not sheriff. I'm a glorified meter reader, Nebraska."

The young man laughed.

"How's your new job?"

"Good...or at least the money's pretty good. Job's not so exciting. I don't know why I ever got into wealth advising."

Pilate grunted as he turned the final screw, which the door didn't take so easily. "Well, financial advisors are necessary," Pilate climbed up, dusted off his trousers, and reached for his level. "Shit, if I had any money, I'd hire you."

"Yeah? Well, about that, I wondered why you're sheriff now...er, I mean constable or whatever. I figured a bestselling book would have carried you to a place of financial freedom."

"Ha! Even if the publisher hadn't run off with my first round of royalties, I'd still need to have some other income, unless it had great paperback and maybe movie rights. It's a misconception that writers are wealthy people who can sit around in their high-priced smoking jackets, collecting checks for every word they write. Living comfortably off one book, even a bestseller, is more rare than a Sasquatch sighting in New York City, barring Times Square."

"Hmm. Well, if you don't mind, what happened?" he asked, clearing his throat. "I mean, you said they ran off with your royalties."

Pilate explained what Frechette did and elaborated on his plans to get the money back.

"Wow," Riley said. "That sucks."

"It does," Pilate said, checking the level. "Almost perfect." Pilate got under the door again, loosened the brackets on one side, and wedged a shim between the post and the door. After screwing the door back to the brackets, he checked the level again. "Damn it." Pilate adjusted the shim for a few more minutes until it met his specifications.

"This is some door," Riley said, standing back and admiring it.

"Bar. It's a bar now," Pilate said. "Well, almost. I need to apply some stain and urethane to the top. You twenty-one yet, Riley?"

"Just last month."

"Well, I can't consider it an official christening or anything, but I've got some Modelos in the fridge," he said.

"I'd like that, Mr. Pilate," he said.

"John. Call me 'John,' Nebraska."

The young man smiled. "Or maybe…'Constable Pilate'?"

"Ass." Pilate laughed.

"Now that I think about it, I guess I'll have to pass on that beer for now. I gotta pick up Abbey."

"Ooh. Hot date?"

"Uh…yeah, I suppose." His face darkened. "Well, no, not really. It's just…well…"

"What's up?"

"Well, Mr…er, John," he stuttered, "that's hard to say."

"'John' is hard to say?"

"No. I mean, yes. Well, that and what I'm thinkin'." Riley crossed and uncrossed his arms. "It's Abbey."

"I thought you said you guys are okay." Pilate wiped his hands on an old shop cloth.

"Yeah, we are, I guess. It's just that...well, I've been in Lincoln for a couple months now, and she's here, and..." Riley looked out over the denuded cornfield, as if he were searching for the words among the stray, dead stalks.

"And you want to get to know other young ladies?"

Riley turned his downcast face away, then back to Pilate. "Yes. I mean, I love Abbey, but I'm just not sure I'm ready for more than dating right now."

"In other words, Riley has discovered that screwing girls in Lincoln is more fun than screwing a curvy hometown school marm." Simon snickered.

"Well, Riley," Pilate said, leaning against the door-turned-bar and picking up his level, "you see this level?"

Riley nodded. "Yeah."

"It requires a lot of effort to hold it perfectly straight, right? To keep that little bubble right there in the middle?"

"Yeah."

"Not too much on this side," he said, moving the level, "or this side." He moved it the opposite way.

"Okay..."

"Relationships are like that. Both people have to feel equal, and everything has to balance out. See?"

Riley smirked. "Kinda corny, but I get what you're saying."

"Okay, let me lay it out for ya. You care about Abbey, but she's content to be a small-town schoolteacher. You're a big--well, sorta big--city finance dude. You see a world of possibilities, and you want to try those out."

He nodded. "Is that bad?"

"Hell no!" Pilate said. "You'd be crazy if you weren't tempted."

"So what do I do?"

"Do you have another girl?"

"Not exactly." He looked down at his sneakers.

"Okay." Pilate lowered his voice. "So you screwed somebody in Lincoln, and you feel terrible about it?"

"What if I screwed somebody in Lincoln and *don't* feel terrible about it? Does that make me crazy...or bad?"

Pilate whistled, long and low. "Well, no, but it does give you your answer. Just do Abbey the courtesy of letting her get on with her life. It isn't fair to string her along. Don't tell her you were doing the bed sheet boogie with somebody else, but you must be honest and let her know you've had a change of heart. She deserves her dignity, as everyone does."

"I don't wanna hurt her. I never did," Riley said, his eyes meeting Pilate's.

"Most guys don't mean to," he said, looking up at Kate as she exited the back door with a cardboard box full of tiki lights. "It's just the way we are sometimes, the nature of the beast. Nothing's always black or white. As much as we wish everything was cut and dry, we live our lives mostly in shades of gray. Women can be the same, believe it or not."

"Wait. I thought we were talking balance, not colors. You make no sense, John," Simon said.

"You won't tell anybody, right?"

"'Course not, Nebraska," Pilate said, offering his hand to seal his word.

Riley's firm, strong grip undoubtedly went a long way toward putting his financial advisement clients at ease, Pilate surmised as he shook his hand.

"Just work on keeping it all level." Pilate clapped his young helper on the back. "And don't beat yourself up about it."

* * *

"What's this?" Pilate asked, holding up a box from UPS. "Taters here already?"

"Ha. I dunno. Came today," Kate said, playing peek-a-boo with Peter.

Pilate opened it and spotted a pair of scuffed brown, square-toed Ariat boots. "Oh my God."

"Whoa, cowboy." Kate laughed. "You ordered boots?"

"Hell no! They're from Mom and Dad. I left them there when I moved up here. I told Dad to give 'em to Goodwill."

"Oh, so that's what he meant!" Kate said.

"Huh?"

"When he called the other day, I told your dad about your new lawman gig, and he said you'd need proper attire."

Pilate sighed.

"Put 'em on," Kate said. "I've never seen you in boots."

"I swore when I left Oklahoma that I was done with all that shit," Pilate said, shoving the atrocities roughly back in the box.

"I don't know," she said, her eyes regarding him warmly. "I've always loved men in boots."

"Am I inferring correctly? If I don these Western fiascos, I might just get…stampeded?"

She grinned. "Ya never know. Maybe I'll make my home, home on your range," she teased.

Pilate smiled back and quickly shoved his feet into the country footwear.

* * *

Pilate looked at the old boots as he urinated, shaking his head. Surprisingly, they did make him feel taller.

"You can take the boy out of Oklahoma, but you can't take the redneck outta the boy," Simon insulted.

Finished, he buttoned his pants and turned on the tap to wash his hands. The restroom at the constable's office was tiny, with just enough room for a man to do his business, turn around to wash up, then step back to open the door to exit. A cracked mirror hung crookedly above the chipped porcelain sink.

Pilate glanced at his reflection, surprised. In his khaki shirt with a Cross Township patch on the left sleeve, his brass constable badge hanging almost as crookedly on his shirt as the mirror on the wall, he didn't look as ridiculous as he felt. He took in the reflection of his face. Lines had formed around his eyes and mouth, and flecks of silver had taken root at his temples, taunting his fleeting youth.

"Scary, isn't it?" Simon said, his face looking over Pilate's shoulder.

Pilate hadn't seen his doppelganger's face in months, though he'd been privy to his mocking voice far more times than he wanted to count. *What's scary?* Pilate's thoughts inquired.

"Responsibility...maturity," Simon said without mirth. *"Look at you. You have kids, a wife, a badge."*

Yeah.

"What happened to you, John? You used to be a lot more fun. Now look at you, a dogcatcher--"

"Constable," Pilate corrected aloud. He turned off the tap and shook his hands to dry them, since the room was sans paper towels and there was no room for an electric dryer.

"Whatever," Simon said. *"You're a bestselling author and were even an honest-to-God hero once. Now you keep little kids from crapping on old ladies' lawns. You're a dogcatcher, for Christ's sake. There are Boy Scouts with more authority than you."*

Maybe.

"Don't go dismissing me with that passive-aggressive agreement nonsense! What would your precious shrink say? Besides, that's no fun." Simon lit a cigarette.

No smoking.

"One of us has to, and you're off running races and doing all that healthy living, though I see you like your drinkies more and more."

A cocktail or glass of wine every week isn't--

"Every week? Pssh. Don't you mean every night? You drink every day, John."

You would, too, if you were me.

"John, like it or not, I am you. You are me, and we are--"

"Constable? You back there?" interrupted a voice from the front office.

"Yeah. Just a minute," Pilate said, wiping his hands on the butt of his Levi's.

Simon waved with his fingers, clicked his tongue, and vanished from the mirror. His cigarette hung in the air for an extra second before disappearing after him.

Pilate turned, pulled the chain on the light, and walked past the jail cell/break room, into the outer area, where his desk was situated.

A youngish man with thinning hair, dressed in an ill-fitting gray suit and fancy burgundy cowboy boots, extended his hand. "Parker."

"Mr. Parker? Nice to meet you."

"Nemec," the man said, making a no-you-don't-understand gesture with his hand.

"I'm sorry?"

"Nemec, Parker Nemec. I'm the bank president," he said, smiling and jerking his thumb over his shoulder. "Next door."

"Oh yes! Of course, Mr. Nemec."

"Parker."

"Parker, yes. Please have a seat. What can I do ya for?"

"Easy, there, Sheriff Taylor," Simon snarked.

Nemec plopped down in the worn chair before the desk.

Pilate slid into Ollie Olafson's comfortable old leather swivel behind the desk.

"Just a social call really," Nemec said. "Just wanted to welcome ya. Nice to, uh…have a celebrity neighbor."

Pilate smiled, wan and dismissive but not unpleasant. "Well, that's kind of you to say, but I'm only warming the chair till they elect a real sheriff."

"You're not gonna run?"

"God no!" Pilate said, as if it was the most absurd notion anyone had ever had.

"Well, I just figured with all your unofficial law enforcement activities since you moved here that you might have a knack for it. When I heard that Jeremy Ryder tapped you for constable, I figured you'd found your true vocation."

"Not even close," Pilate said. "I just need to make a little extra money, and it's a chance to help the community out."

Nemec cracked his knuckles, an absentminded habit he was unaware he often performed. "Is there anything the bank can do for you?"

"Not unless you've got some free money lying around."

"Ha! 'Fraid not. I just meant if you need a place to put your book royalties or want to refinance your farm--"

"Thanks, Parker. That's mighty nice of you. Kate handles most of that, but I'll let her know you offered."

Nemec looked suddenly deflated, as if he was stuck on a subway and fighting a bad case of the trots.

"Anything I can do for you folks at the bank?"

The banker shook his head. "No, no, we're good. Haven't been robbed in…well, ever. Ollie being next door sorta stifled that kind of thing."

"I imagine so. Well, I hope my presence will be something of a deterrent too," Pilate said, "though I'm not really here much."

"And I see you don't pack any heat," Nemec said.

Pilate shook his head. "Guns get people hurt or worse. I'm not much more than a glorified meter maid anyway. No need."

"You'd be surprised."

"Actually, I wouldn't." Pilate looked at the banker curiously, wondering why the nervous man, who knows full well of Pilate's run-ins with the criminal element in Cross, would say something so clueless.

"Yeah, I guess you wouldn't," Nemec said. He looked over Pilate's shoulder. "Ollie used to have a big carving of an eagle hanging on the wall back there. Looked a little spooky, always seemed to be staring right through people."

"I figure Ollie was spooky enough on his own," Pilate said quietly. He felt odd talking so casually about the man he had killed in self-defense, especially since he was currently dusting the man's chair with his own ass.

"There are worse things," Nemec said quietly, keeping his eyes on the desk.

"I'm sorry?"

"Nothin'. Say, I don't mean to step on any tender toes, but you, uh… You were friends with Derek Krall, right? I mean, before he--"

"Before he blackmailed half the town and tried to get me killed? Yeah."

"Sorry. I just was thinking about him the other day," Nemec said, his eyes darting to the side.

"Oh? Any reason why?"

"I was over at the college library, doing a little research, so of course he came to mind. We were friends, too, till his criminal enterprises came to light."

"That's understandable. Derek was an interesting and pretty likable guy, for a lying sack of crap. But you were doing research?" Pilate said.

"Oh," the banker said, waving a dismissive hand, "I'm just something of an ol' history buff. Derek did bad things, of course, but he was a great librarian and town historian, so when I'm looking for anything about county history, I start there. Google has nothing on him."

"I see," Pilate said. "Anything in particular?"

"Just some bits and pieces about downtown. I always get questions about the town history from tourists during OakFest, so I was readying up. Anyway…" He slapped his palms on his knees and stood. "I've already talked your ear off. I'd better be going, Constable. Just let me know if there's anything I can ever do for you."

Pilate shook Nemec's clammy hand. "Certainly," he said, then walked him out to the sidewalk.

"Pretty day. I like autumn," Nemec said.

Pilate gestured across the wide main street. "Me too."

"And OakFest is a-comin' up," Nemec said, nodding.

"Yeah, lotsa fun. I imagine I'll have to restrain myself from writing too many parking tickets."

Nemec chuckled and nodded again.

For a moment, both men fell silent.

Pilate searched for something to say. "Um, hey, is anybody ever gonna reopen Mostek's General Store?" he asked, gesturing across the street to the abandoned building. "We need a place to get groceries besides the c-store, and my wife's tired of making the long haul to Goss City."

Nemec nodded hurriedly. "Yeah, it could be a real gold mine for the right buyer. There are a couple interested parties."

"Oh? Who?"

"Well, I'm not at liberty to say. Mrs. Mostek, in light of Perry's disappearance and the shooting of Sheriff Welliver…well, the poor thing can't bear to step foot back in there. She wants to sell soon as possible."

"Well, I hope somebody buys it quickly," Pilate said. "Great meeting you, Parker."

Nemec flashed a quick grin and nodded, then traversed the ten feet to the bank door, nestled between two faux ionic pillars.

Pilate looked down the deserted street. The Cross College carillon echoed, announcing that it was five o'clock. The town tavern would soon fill with thirsty patrons, and Constable Pilate would likely have to roust a few drunks before the night was through.

Dogcatcher? Yup. That's me.

Chapter Eleven

Professor Harley Cordwainer barked through the phone at Pilate, literally: "*Bark, bark, bark*! I can't freaking stand it," he said. "All night long, the incessant yapping of that four-legged mange magnet, that grotesque perversion of genetics. Have you even seen this animal? Part husky, part Chihuahua. His legs are so short that his scraggly dick drags in the dirt, like somebody strapped a flashlight-sized lipstick to a mutated rat."

Pilate burst into laughter, which he quickly morphed into a cough. "Professor, what would you have me do?"

"Go over to Mrs. Drum's house and shoot that escapee from the damn island of Dr. Moreau," he said, his voice high-pitched and quickly running out of steam.

"Professor, please," Pilate said. "Mrs. Drum already has issues with someone fouling her yard, and--"

"That's not my concern. Listen up, Mr. *New York Times* Bestselling Dogcatcher, if you don't do somethin' to make that mutt stop yapping at all hours, I'll see you in court." With that, Cordwainer slammed his black phone down on its cradle.

Pilate winced, chuckled, and put down the receiver. Now he had the crankiest and most litigious professor at Cross College mad at him. "Just what I need," he mumbled.

The late Dean Trevathan told Pilate about Cordwainer in an offhanded conversation after first sighting the short, stocky, gray little man in the cafeteria. Trevathan recommended then that Pilate give Cordwainer a wide berth, unless Cordwainer appeared to be in the midst of one of those rare months when he was on his meds. "Cordwainer is the classic pain in the ass," Trevathan had said, his good eye twinkling.

Tenured, privileged, and talented; twice nominated and once a winner of a Hugo award; and thrice nominated for an Edgar, Harley Cordwainer was, at one time, considered a true force in genre fiction. In the 1970s, he was often mentioned in the same breath as Heinlein and Asimov.

Pilate remembered reading Cordwainer's work. His science fiction was bleak, funny, rarely hopeful, scattered, and marvelous. His mystery novels were stuffed with luxuriant prose and confusing but perfectly entwined plot twists. Young Pilate never would have dreamt he'd actually meet the man, let alone be threatened with a lawsuit by the legendary scribbler.

Pilate asked Trevathan how such a literary luminary had ended up in the smallest town in the world, to which Trevathan merely shrugged and said, "He's an asshole. Can't get along with anybody anywhere else. This is the end of the road for him. I doubt he can write anymore either. All he does is talk about his 'precious,' which I assume is some manuscript that only exists in his swollen head. Who gives a shit though, as long as his classes are full?"

Pilate figured something had hobbled Cordwainer, like a stone in his shoe along the way to Cross. *Perhaps it was the fifth divorce or the three famously unfinished novels and subsequent returned advances.* Whatever the reason, once-promising genius Harley Cordwainer limped off the humongous world stage into minuscule Cross, sentencing himself to teaching creative writing and shouting to the heavens about perceived affronts to his character.

"Had enough yet?" Simon said.

Yet? I had enough a long, long time ago.

"Pity, pity!" Simon said.

Shut up.

"Boy, you're grouchy when you're a laughingstock."

Pilate began to formulate a worthy comeback to his own mind, but a man walked in the office before he could conjure one.

"Constable Pilate?" The man was young, maybe thirty, with a crew cut, wide, dark eyes, and pale skin. He was dressed quite casually in a green Army fatigues jacket, jeans, and blue Puma sneakers.

"Yes." Pilate had seen him around; it would have been odd not to in such a small spot on the map.

"I'm Gary Rich, Cross Township Neighborhood Watch Captain," he said. "You can call me Gary though."

"As opposed to?"

"Captain."

"He looks serious. Oh my God. He is!" Simon said.

"Oh. Well, thank you, Gary. Of course you can call me 'John,'" Pilate said, gesturing for Neighborhood Watch Captain Gary Rich to take a seat. "What can I do ya for?"

"Stop saying that, you idiot," Simon said. *"It's as outdated and stupid as this guy's shoes."*

Rich sat down, reaching simultaneously into his jacket, and removed a small notebook. "Well, now that you are the constable…" He sighed, looking at the ceiling and swallowing hard enough to make his Adam's Apple protrude. "I didn't even know the job was open."

"Why?" Pilate snorted. "You want it?"

Rich's eyes grew wider. "Really?"

"Kidding, but the seat will probably be vacant a while after a new sheriff is sworn in. That's assuming the position isn't abolished."

"Well, even after the new sheriff comes, shouldn't they keep the position filled?"

Pilate shrugged. "Take it up with Jeremy Ryder, over at the county office."

Rich sagged in his chair. "Doesn't return my calls. See if I'll vote for him again." Rich opened his spiral notepad, licked his index finger, and flipped quickly through pages, until he found what he was looking for. "I wanna let you know that neighborhood watch is on the job."

"That's great. How many of you are there?"

Rich's eyes rolled up, looking left. "Oh, there're two or three… Eight or ten, really, though I handle most of it 'cause I have the most time."

"Oh?"

"I'm on disability." He pointed at corporal's stripes on his Army jacket sleeve.

"Combat?"

"Well, sort of. I mean, I coulda been shipped out. I was National Guard, but I fell off a ladder while I was painting the barracks, and I severely hurt my back. Uncle Sam didn't have no use for me then."

"Well, the important thing is that you served," Pilate said.

"Did you?"

Pilate shook his head. "No, and I regret it. I wish I'da spent a few years doing my bit. I guess being constable is my contribution. The pay is certainly not any better than the Army." Pilate attempted a laugh, but it was met by Rich's unblinking, blank stare.

"You're sadly contemptible, John," Simon said.

Rich looked back at his notepad. "Constable, we have some issues that need to be dealt with."

"Okay. Shoot."

"This should be good," Simon said. *"Need a drink, Johnny boy?"*

Rich thumbed a page back, then looked at the notebook again. "Okay. Well, it seems there's some…harassment going on."

Pilate leaned forward in his chair, reaching for his notepad and pen. "Go on."

"Okay, well, I live over on Live Oak and Tenth. You know it?"

Pilate knew it well, for it wasn't far from the road that led to Monticello Cemetery, up on the hill. Monticello Cemetery was home to the town's dead, going back nearly 200 years. It was the scene of Pilate's defeat of Jack Lindstrom, the psychopathic past president of Cross College. So, he nodded.

"Well, here's the deal. I walk my dog there. Oscar. He's a wiener dog."

"Oscar? As in…Oscar Mayer, the wiener-makers? Really? Stop! I-I can't take it," Simon mumbled in Pilate's frontal lobe.

"And…" Pilate prodded, holding his hand to his chin and covering his lips with his finger so a giggle would not escape.

"Well, every day when we get to the corner of the street, right at the stop sign for the last three weeks, I've found this." Rich reached into one of the large outside jacket pockets and pulled out a plastic baggie, then slapped it down on Pilate's desk.

Pilate picked it up at the corner with two fingers and held it up to the light. Inside the baggie was a crumpled beer can.

"Same cheap brand, always crushed, always left on that corner. There are usually two or three of them, just lying there."

Pilate carefully laid the baggie-encased can on his desk. "I'm not sure I follow."

"Isn't it obvious?" Rich asked, incredulous.

Pilate shrugged.

"Harassment, John! Somebody's leaving these cans there to harass me."

"John, whoever is paying this guy is brilliant. You're getting punked," Simon drawled.

"Well, littering is against code, but I'm not sure it's harassment."

"Of course it is," Rich said. "Ever since I put flyers on the doors in my neighborhood warning of unacceptable behavior, this started."

"Unacceptable behavior?"

"Yes. After all the violence lately..." He looked away from Pilate, to the can on Pilate's desk. "You know all about that. But anyway..." He looked back at the constable. "When the sheriff was put out of commission, I stepped up and started the neighborhood watch. I wanted to put everyone on notice that there are statutes against loud music, leaving your trashcans on the curb, parking on the wrong side of the street, and--"

"Littering?"

His head bobbed with excitement. "You see?"

"So you put flyers on doors, warning people that you are watching?"

"Yes. Crime is everyone's problem, and fighting it is everyone's job. With no sheriff onboard, somebody had to do something. Then, like I said, the very next day, these beer cans started appearing on the corner by my house."

"And you think it's a harassment, somebody trying to get back at you for your...crime-fighting efforts?"

"Yes! Somebody is dumping these cans by my lawn, and I want you to help me catch them. I stayed up late last night and the night before, but I didn't see anybody."

"Yet the cans were there in the morning?"

"Yes. I...well, I guess I dozed off sometime around eleven," he said, downcast.

"And what is it that you want me to do?" Pilate asked, making notes.

"Dust for prints," he said. "I picked up the can with a pencil, through the opening. Ya know, you might even be able to get DNA off the mouth of the can."

"Cuckoo. Cuckoo," Simon added.

"Mr. Rich…Gary…" Pilate started.

"Yes?"

"I don't even have a fingerprinting kit," Pilate explained, straining not to laugh. "Even if I did, I have no idea how to lift prints, and DNA testing is a very expensive process."

"Well, I'm a citizen, and my rights are being violated," Rich said.

"Mr. Rich, you *are* the victim--and that's a strong word--of a serial litterer, to be sure. But this is a college town. I suspect it's a case of students drinking a few beers as they cruise town, then dropping the empties at the stop sign, which just so happens to be your corner."

"But I--"

Pilate held up a hand. "Let me finish. I bet if you look at every other intersection in town, you're likely to find similar litter from time to time, possibly even the same brand."

"So you're not going to check this out?"

"I will log your complaint and keep an eye out. If you spot the, uh… culprit, get a license plate number and call me. I'll talk to them."

"That's it?" Rich said.

"What else can I do?"

He stood, his face flushed. "Constable, I have to put you on notice right now that you are a major disappointment. Also, since this borders on dereliction of duty, I may run against you for this job when it comes open."

Pilate stood. "Mr. Rich, I'm doing all I can do within the budget and legal parameters of this job. If you want the job, it's all yours, as soon as the county commissioners decide to open it up for election. As it stands now, that should be in two years, as I'm finishing a vacated term."

"John, that's a bald-faced lie," Simon said, *"but it's pretty funny."*

"We'll see about that," Rich said, walking to the door.

"Captain Rich…"

He turned around, one hand on the doorknob.

"No more flyers putting people on notice, if you please."

Rich shook his head slowly. "I am responsible for my neighborhood's safety."

"Actually, I am. Let me do my job. You can help me by reporting suspicious behavior, but riling up the neighbors won't do any good."

"Reporting it? Pssh. If I see those punks, I'm gonna put 'em under citizen's arrest," he said, pointing at the floor.

Pilate raised his voice. "You will do no such thing, Mr. Rich. That is a direct order from your duly appointed peace officer. You are not empowered to enforce laws. You are to report lawbreaking to the sheriff or me. I mean, after we get a new sheriff. Report it to me for now. Do you understand?"

"Fine." He pivoted on the ball of his foot and stormed out, then slammed the glass door as hard as he could.

"Don't forget your can."

* * *

Sipping a martini in the moonlight, Pilate leaned against his front door, now horizontal and in his backyard. A cool breeze wafted by. He looked at the house and saw lights on in Peter's nursery and Kara's room.

He glimpsed Kate, placing little Peter in his crib, the shadow playing on the wall until she turned off the light. A moment later, Kara's light went off, the soft glow of her nightlight all that remained.

Pilate took another sip.

"Too much vermouth," Simon opined. *"No Lillet in this wide spot in the road."*

The back door opened quietly, and Kate leaned out, trying to make out if Pilate was in the backyard. She switched on the floodlight, making his eyes contract painfully. She turned the flood off and ambled over to him, wearing a t-shirt she'd picked up in Key West; it said "Beach or Bust" across the front.

"I'll take bust," Pilate flirted.

"Ha! That one never gets old. On a stakeout, Officer?" she asked, kissing his cheek.

"Just unwinding at my favorite bar," he answered.

"Dark out here," Kate said, kissing him again, this time on the mouth. "You know, it's better when two people do it."

He kissed her back. "Sorry, babe."

"That's okay." She picked up his glass and sipped it. "Yuck! Too much vermouth."

"I know. I was in a hurry. Didn't want the kids to hear me and try to stay up."

"Thank you."

"Welcome."

"Long day?"

"Well…" He sighed. "Let's just say there're a lot of interesting folks in this town."

"You don't gotta tell me that," she said, wrapping her arms around his waist and leaning her head against his shoulder. "Have I thanked you lately?"

"For what?"

"For being such a stand-up guy about all this."

"All of what?" he asked, even though he knew the answer.

"You coulda freaked out about losing the book money and having to take this shitty job, but you didn't."

"There's still time."

She laughed quietly into his neck. "The John Pilate I met last year probably would have. You've really changed, John."

"Is that good? I mean, is it okay?"

"Of course! Why would you even ask that?" She pulled away, searching in the darkness for his eyes. A cloud moved, allowing some moonlight to dance between them.

"Some people don't like change. They want people they marry or work with or whatever to stay the same. Change scares people."

She nodded. "I get that, but I love the guy you are now. I don't think I want the depressed, womanizing, scattered John Pilate back."

"Some people do," Simon said.

"You left out entertaining, sexy, and charming."

"You're still sexy and charming. You're just…maturing."

"What an awful thing to say," he said in mock apprehension.

"The truth hurts. You're growing up."

"Speaking of entertaining…uh, when do you think we'll get back to that on a regular basis?"

"Let's see. Peter will graduate high school in seventeen and a half years, and--"

"Stop! It sucks to grow up."

"Sorry."

Pilate sipped took another small sip of his drink, then placed the Nick-and-Nora-style martini glass on the bar. "Kate, does it…"

She looked him right in the face. "What?"

"I mean, having kids," he said. "I just feel like I have to protect them all the time, like all I do is look out for them. You know, like baby-proofing the house and packing throw pillows around the coffee table when Pete's wallowing around the living room. I just feel like I have to always be here, like I have to make sure they're safe."

"That's just part of being a parent," she said, chuckling, "and a good one at that."

"Is it really just that, or do you think it's some kinda post-traumatic stress thing from all the crap we've been through? I mean, I think about those kids constantly. Is that normal?"

She nodded. "Oh yeah. Before I had Kara, somebody told me I'd never have another carefree moment in my life. They were right."

"That really sucks." He reached for the martini.

"It's all right, John. It's life, and it forces you to behave and take fewer stupid risks."

"Yet I'm the dogcatcher," he said.

"I said take fewer risks, not become a complete bore."

"A mature dogcatcher? Kate, that's boring."

"Well, yeah, maybe a little," she said, "but I think we've all had enough adventure for a while, wouldn't you say?"

Somewhere in his consciousness, Pilate heard an echo of Simon cackling.

"Kate?"

"Yeah?"

"I'm wearing my boots."

Chapter Twelve

Pilate finished his fried eggs and buttered wheat toast, gulped down coffee, and put his dishes in the sink.

In the living room, Peter was nestled on his mother's chest, drinking a bottle.

"Hey, little man," Pilate said, kissing them both. "Where's Kara?"

"Brushing her teeth. Hey, did you go running this morning?"

"Yeah, just a couple miles. The boots make it tough."

"Ha! Good though. Wish I could. Anyway, Kara missed her ride with the neighbors, so..."

"It's okay. I'll drop her off on my way."

"Process service?" Kate asked, adjusting the burp cloth on her shoulder.

He nodded. "Hey, I get mileage with those, so it's a banner day."

Kate smirked. "Have you called Monique lately? Maybe she's heard something."

"I'll make a note," he said, pinning on his badge.

"Lopsided."

"God, I hate this thing," he said, trying to correct it. "Where's my level?"

"When does Taters get in?"

"I'm picking him up at the airport tomorrow, at ten thirty," Pilate said. "That's why I want to get this service out of the way, so I don't have to screw with it while he's here."

Kara bounded downstairs, made a few googly eyes at her little brother, and kissed him and Kate. "Bye-bye!"

"Bye, sweetie. Have a great day," Kate said.

"C'mon, you little toot," Pilate said.

"I'm not a little toot, Daddy." Kara folded her arms and stuck her bottom lip out in a pout.

"Sorry, but you are." Pilate tickled her.

She giggled and ran to the door.

* * *

As they passed Cross College on the way to the school, Kara gazed out the backseat window. "That's where that bad man tried to hurt you."

"Well, yes," Pilate said, glancing out the window. "But that's all over now, and the place isn't bad. Mommy and I teach there."

"Uh-uh. You don't teach school. You have a new job."

"Yes, well, the new job is temporary."

"What does temprayery mean?"

"For a short time." He was interrupted by a dinging sound. "Hey, is your seatbelt on, squirt?" Pilate asked, looking at Kara in the rearview mirror.

"Oh. No. Sorry." She scrabbled for the seatbelt.

"Kara, what have I told you about unbuckling it?"

"Sorry, Daddy. I was trying to see out the window better."

"Kara, do you know what my real job is?"

"Uh, um...teacher?"

"Sort of, but not really. Guess again."

"Book writer?"

"Yes, but there's one job that's more important."

"Sheriff?"

"No. That's close, but it's not the most important job."

"What is your most important job, Daddy?"

"To keep you safe."

Kara smiled in the back seat. He had told her the same thing many times, but she never seemed to tire of hearing it.

"And Peter and Mommy too?"

"Yep, that's my job, to keep you safe, and I can't do that if you're not wearing your seatbelt."

"Or if one of any number of psychos come out of the woodwork in this mutated Mayberry," Simon said.

Pilate pulled up to Kara's school, where a hundred kids from five different grades were swarming all about.

Standing in front of the building was Abbey, his former student, now a teacher. "Hey there Mr…er, John," she said, smiling.

"Hey, Abbey," he said, leaning over the passenger side to let Kara out.

"Bye, Daddy," Kara said, running inside.

"Bye, sweet girl," he said.

"Growing up fast," Abbey said. "How's your Peter?"

"My what?"

"Uh…your son. How's your *son* Peter?" she said, blushing.

"Oh. He's fine," he said.

"Good." Abbey gently nudged a couple students toward the door. "Riley said he helped you fix a door or something."

"Yeah," Pilate said. "He's a good guy."

"Yes, he is," she said, looking down at her shoes. "You know he broke it off with me, right?"

Pilate's smiled faded. "Oh no, Abbey. I didn't know."

"He said he just needs a little time," she said, wiping a tear and breathing in noisily. "It's okay though. I figured when he moved to Lincoln he might get the wandering eye."

"Abbey, he's nuts if he does that," Pilate said.

"What a two-faced jerk you are, John," Simon said.

"No, really, he's okay. I can't blame him."

"Well, give it a little time," he said. "He'll come to his senses and be back."

She shook her head quickly, inhaled, and forced a smile. "Will do."

The bell rang.

"That's my cue. Better go," she said. "See you around, Mr. Pilate."

* * *

He checked the subpoena again. The Tin Roof Rib Shack was being sued for back taxes, so it fell to Pilate to serve Bart Robeson's court papers. Pilate cruised past a few farm trucks, giving the customary four-fingered wave from his steering wheel as they went by. It was a chilly day, making Pilate grateful for the old Saab's seat warmers as he blew down the road, orange and brown leaves flying in his wake.

Hilmer Thurman's Brown Betty Roadhouse appeared in the distance, with the usual three or four pickups and beat-up cars parked haphazardly in front.

Glad I have no business there today.

"Yes, a man can take only so much backwoods mafia talk," Simon sarcastically agreed.

Thurman had kept a low profile since taking over his dead cousin Ollie's criminal enterprises. He didn't throw his weight around, and even when Jeremy Ryder named Pilate constable, the Olafson clan didn't speak a word about it. Where Olafson had been showy and intemperate and reckless, Thurman was quiet, calm, and resolute.

Perhaps that made him more dangerous, Pilate considered.

Sweet, delicious smoke from the Tin Roof Rib Shack lured Pilate out of his thoughts. He pulled onto the gravel outside the building, which truly was a tin shack. Smoke drifted from behind cords of wood in back.

Pilate picked up the paperwork from the passenger seat, checked to make sure his stubborn badge was on straight and strode to the door.

He raised his hand to knock but was interrupted by a black man in his late twenties, with a thin, scraggly beard. He was carrying a large axe, sweating profusely in the cool air.

"Help you?" the man asked, hefting the axe.

Pilate cleared his throat. "John Pilate, Cross Township Constable. Are you Bartholomew Paul Robeson?"

The man shook his head. "Nope. What can I do ya for?"

"See? That's how dumb you sound when you say that," Simon said.

"I need to speak with Mr. Robeson about a legal matter."

"He under arrest?"

"No, nothing like that. Can you tell me if he's inside?"

The man shook his head, and the axe blade glinted in the sun. "I can tell 'im you come by."

"Are you open?" Pilate asked, gesturing at the door.

"Nope, not till noon."

"Well, is Mr. Robeson nearby? I really need to talk to him today."

The man shrugged, turning the axe handle in his palms, rotating the blade.

"Nice cutlery," Simon said.

"Well, who cooks and takes care of the customers?"

"I do, and Melba and Cinnamon Tate."

"So you're telling me Mr. Robeson isn't here to run his own restaurant?"

"Restaurant?" He snorted. "Whatever, mister."

"What's your name?"

"Why? Am I under arrest?"

"No, you're not."

"You can call me Mistah Tibbs."

"Okay." Pilate managed a dry, raspy chuckle. "Mr. Tibbs. Uh-huh. I'll just come by some other time and see if I can catch Mr. Robeson."

"I'll be sure to tell 'im you was here, Sheriff."

"Constable."

"What?"

"Constable. It's different than sheriff."

"Okay. If ya say so." He twirled the axe again, shrugged, and wandered back behind the shack.

A few seconds later, Pilate heard the sound of the axe striking wood.

* * *

Pilate checked his watch and saw that it was eleven a.m. He started to pass the Brown Betty, then slowed, did a u-turn and parked in front of the roadhouse.

"What the hell are you doing?" Simon asked.

A little police work.

"A little dogcatching, Constable?"

Pilate walked into the bar, startling three daytime boozers who were nursing their Buds. His eyes adjusted to the dim lighting, and he took in the sight of Nelda, who was standing precariously on a stepladder behind the bar, screwing in a light bulb. "Um, hi," Pilate said.

"Just a minute, honey. Cain't you see I'm screwin'?" Nelda asked, then cackled at her own shameless innuendo.

"Charming," Simon said.

She walked her bony butt down the steps, thin gold bracelets clattering on her wrists as she peeled a sticky cobweb from the light fixture. "What can I do ya for, sheriff?"

Shut up, Simon.

He didn't bother correcting her. "I'm hopin' you can help me. I'm looking for Bart Robeson."

"Oh, honey…" She snapped up a bar rag and wiped the counter absently. "He don't work here. He owns the Tin Roof, down the road. Just follow your nose."

"I know, but I heard he comes by here every now and again, and I just need to chat with him."

"Well, he does, but not today. He's probably at the Tin Roof, gettin' ready for lunch rush. Sometimes he brings a rack or two of ribs and some butt over for us to sell."

"Nelda, I've got this," Hilmer Thurman said, sticking his head out the door of his office. "Hello, Constable. Come on in."

Pilate nodded and walked inside the small office behind Thurman. "Last time I was in here, we had a meeting of the minds," Pilate said as both men sat, Thurman behind his desk, Pilate in a small wooden chair across from him. Though Thurman wasn't smoking, the room reeked of cigars.

Thurman smiled. "That we did."

"I must admit, I didn't expect such a warm welcome today."

"Last time you were in here, you weren't wearing any fancy brass jewelry," Thurman said, nodding at the badge.

"And the last time we talked, it was on the phone. I believe you said we're even."

"Hmm. I don't recollect that."

Pilate nodded.

"So, to what do we owe the honor?"

"I'm hoping to talk to Bart Robeson. He around?"

Thurman smiled. "Sadly, no. I could go for some ribs and slaw right about now. You should try his place down the road. Just follow your--"

"Nose? Yeah, I did. He's apparently not there. Only saw some guy with an axe."

"Otis."

"Mr. Tibbs."

Thurman burst into laughter. "Tibbs? Mr. Tibbs? Love it."

"Yeah, it was funny."

"So, anyway, what do you want with Robie?"

"Well, it's a legal matter."

"Process server, eh? My, how the mighty have fallen," Thurman said between his perfectly straight, white teeth.

Dentures?

"Maybe, but I do get fancy jewelry," Pilate said. He played it cool but felt sweat forming in his armpits.

"What do you want, Constable Pilate?" Thurman said, calm, cool, and unnervingly polite.

"I just hoped I might catch Bart Robeson…and I figured I may as well say hello to you."

"Hi."

Again with the teeth?

"And ask if you've heard from Perry Mostek."

Thurman's face darkened, and the teeth disappeared behind thin, pursed lips. After a couple seconds, he brightened with a well-orchestrated smile, revealing the pearlies that were, most definitely, dentures. "No. Perry blew town after he shot Sheriff Welliver. I can honestly say I haven't seen or heard from him since."

"Well, his wife needs money, and she's putting the store up for sale."

"Yeah, I heard that."

"I figured you might have. You happen to know anybody who's looking to buy it?"

"Maybe, maybe not."

"Well, I spoke with that banker, Mr. Nemec, about it," Pilate said, keeping his scrutinizing eyes on Thurman's face.

Thurman was a fount of pleasantry. "Oh?"

"Yeah. He says there are a couple of interested parties."

Thurman nodded. "I see. Well, it's the only game in town. Whoever gets it will do pretty well. Everybody needs groceries, and they're all sick of driving ten miles to get 'em in Goss City."

"Me included," Pilate said, standing. "Well, thanks for your time."

"You bet, Constable," Thurman said, leaning back in his chair. "Oh, how's your family doing?"

Pilate clenched his jaw. "They're fine."

"Good, good. Pretty rough, that car accident your wife had a while back."

"Thanks for helping out," Pilate said. Thurman had found Kate's wrecked station wagon hanging precariously off a bridge. He may have saved her life and the life of their unborn baby by calling for an ambulance.

"Least I could do. Hope that never happens again," Thurman said. "Terrible to contemplate."

Pilate opened the door. "Yeah, that's for sure."

"Well, as long as people take care, accidents don't happen."

"Goodbye, Mr. Thurman," Pilate said. His knees felt funny, his guts hot and sickening.

"I'll tell Robie you're lookin' for him," Thurman called after Pilate.

* * *

Back in his office, Pilate saw the blinking light indicating that a message had been left on his voicemail. He pushed the playback button and listened closely.

"You really need to get a decent cell phone," Jeremy Ryder drawled.

"I have one," Pilate told the machine, looking at his cell, only to realize it was set on vibrate.

"Look, I heard Gary Rich came by and that you used your world-famous charm on him. Can you please smooth that guy out so I don't have to hear about serial littering or whatever the hell he's got up his nosy ass? By the way, I also heard that Jim Kolar over in Vettsville is thinkin' of throwing his hat in the ring for sheriff. That's a good one, right? Talk at ya."

Click.

Pilate didn't know Kolar personally, but his friend, State Trooper Hulsey, had mentioned him once, referring to Kolar as a "solid, stand-up guy."

Pilate sighed as he pondered the neighborhood watch captain calling Ryder to complain about Pilate's lack of interest in his ridiculous, unfounded suspicions.

Beep.

"Sheriff, this is Mrs. Drum. That boy pooped in my yard again. What are you gonna do about it? Please come over and look at this poop. If I catch the little twerp, I'm gonna put a cork where the sun don't shine!"

Beep.

"Harley Cordwainer here. I was up all night listening to that yappy homunculus. If you don't do something about it, I will."

Beep.

"Constable, this is Watch Captain Rich. I saw a strange man riding his bike by my house last night, around seven. He wouldn't make eye contact. I think he's up to something, maybe drugs. He's Mexican, I think. I need to file a report."

Beep.

Pilate fell heavily into his chair, holding his face in his hands.

Chapter Thirteen

"Why in the hell is the airport so far away?" Taters Malley stared balefully out the Saab window. "We've been driving for half an hour."

"We live in one of the armpits of the state. Omaha is the nearest national airport, unless you take a private charter and land in the next county over, something I'd rather you didn't, considering recent events."

Taters looked at Pilate. "Right. That nut-job ex-president dude hijacked a small plane to get here, didn't he? Sorry."

"How's Jordan?"

"Beautiful, more woman than I deserve and more man than I'll ever be."

Pilate raised his eyebrow.

"I just mean she's ace, brother, just great. She was plenty happy to see me climb on that jet, though, let me tell ya."

"Well, I can't believe we got you away from the *TenFortyEZ*," Pilate said.

"Me neither. I miss 'em both already. The two ladies in my life. Speaking of ladies, how're your girls?"

"Wonderful…and looking forward to seeing you," Pilate said, checking his rearview mirror.

"Peter ruling the roost?"

"Growing like a weed."

"Good."

The pair drove in silence for a few miles.

"How's your ticker?"

Taters snorted. "Fine, fine. Silly nonsense, all of it. I don't mean to sound like one of them conspiracy theorists or whatnot, but personally, I think it's just a way for the insurance companies and hospitals to rob me blind. That's what they do, you know. They find something and blow it all outta proportion so they can run expensive tests, pokin' and proddin' me in places I didn't even know I've got places and then chargin' me an arm and a leg for it. That's the Taters Malley theory on that."

Pilate chuckled. "You're taking your medication, though, right?"

"Yeah. They've got me on all kinds of pills, tons of 'em, in every damn color of the rainbow. They're hoping the meds'll break down some of the blockage so they don't have to crack my chest. Jeez, what is that thing? A tractor?"

"Harvester."

"Wow. Looks like a spaceship. Anyway, in a couple more weeks, I get another multimillion-dollar scan to see if their pretty little pills are doing anything, and they'll decide the next brilliant move then."

"How do you feel?"

"Fine. I get a little tired, but I'm good unless I overexert. It's a real drag as far as the boudoir is concerned, if ya know what I mean."

Pilate nodded. "I can imagine."

"What's the point of havin' a young, gorgeous wife if you can't properly tend to her lady needs?"

"No argument there, T."

"Are we there yet? I really gotta piss. These drugs run right through me."

"We can stop up here," Pilate said.

"They film *Field of Dreams* up here?"

"No. That was in Iowa, I think."

"Close enough," Taters said. "That Susan Sarandon…mmm, mmm, mmm…" He whistled.

"That was *Bull Durham*."

"Oh. Well, whatever. Just please tell me they sell Modelo up here in this overgrown cornfield. If they serve it, I will drink."

* * *

They stopped in Goss City for lunch.

"What the hell kind of salad dressing is this?" Taters asked.

"Dorothy Lynch. Try it," Pilate said, chewing his bison burger. "It's a Nebraska thing."

Taters tasted it and made a face.

"Oh, c'mon. It's not that bad."

"No, it ain't the dressing. It's just salad in general," he said. "Jordan made me go veggie, and it's killin' me just looking at that juicy buffalo burger."

"Bison."

"Same thing, if ya ask me. Whatever it is, this damn rabbit food ain't no comparison."

"I'm sorry," Pilate said. "I wouldn't have ordered it if I had known."

"Well, why should you suffer too?" Taters asked, laughing. "I'm not supposed to drink either, but I'm telling you right now that there'd better be cold ones at your place. Otherwise, there's gonna be trouble no amount of constable peace-officering will prevent."

"There will be beer," Pilate said, wiping his mouth with a cloth napkin.

"How'd you ever end up with that badge anyway? I mean, what the hell? Is it research for a new book?"

"Yes and no," Pilate said, finishing his iced tea.

Taters pushed aside his salad. "Is it complicated?"

"Isn't everything?"

"Yup, especially my ticker," he said. "How much longer till we get to the town time forgot?"

"About twenty minutes, give or take."

"The way you drive, I suspect it'll take a good half-hour."

"There's nothing wrong with safe driving."

"You drive like an old woman."

"You *do* need a beer," Pilate said. "You're grouchy as hell, but it's still good to see you, pal."

"You too," Taters parroted, smiling and wiping his mouth with a napkin. "Now, can we get to Criss-Cross City or whatever you call it so I can see everybody?"

* * *

After a joyful reunion and home-cooked meal with the Pilate family--vegetarian lasagna, much to Taters's chagrin--the old friends wandered out into the back yard.

"Holy shit! What is this?" Taters asked.

"It's the Frontdoor Backyard Bar, of course," Pilate said proudly, reaching under the bar and opening a cooler. He popped the cap off a Modelo and slid it across to Taters.

Taters smiled, picked up the bottle, and waited for Pilate to open his beer. "To my landlocked friend, who is sorely missed."

"To my pirate buddy, who is also missed."

As the pair settled onto a couple of beat-up barstools Pilate had found at a flea market in Brownville, the sun was setting, a visual riot of amber and orange.

"Not the same skies out here, that's for sure," Taters said.

"Yeah, the sunsets are gorgeous here, but I prefer the Green Flash on the Gulf."

"Gotta appreciate what you have," Taters said, "love the one you're with, ya know?"

"True," Pilate said, then finished his bottle. "Want another?"

Taters slugged the rest of it down and nodded.

Pilate popped two more.

"John, you doin' okay here?" For the first time since he arrived, Taters adopted a concerned tone.

"Sure."

"I mean it, buddy. I thought the plan was to get the hell outta Dodge."

"Life is what happens to you while you're busy making other plans," Pilate said, sipping his beer. "The asshole took all my book money, and I've got mouths to feed."

"Apparently, that guy doesn't know you very well. I'd be afraid to take your cash after what you did to the bad guys here."

Pilate looked at the top of the bar.

"Sorry." He pressed his bottle cap into a taco shape. "Why aren't you teaching?"

"Well, besides the fact that the new dean doesn't hold a candle to our friend Trevathan, there are no sections open for me to teach right now."

"But constable? I mean, no offense, but the closest you've ever been to being a cop was screwing that sexy police officer in Key West."

Pilate shushed him.

"Well, it's true," Taters said in a whisper.

"I know that, but I'm not really a cop. I'm more of a…town overlooker."

"Overlooker? Is that even a word?"

"I'm a writer. I can take creative liberties that Webster's can't argue with. But forget that. My job is to keep an eye on things. I do parking tickets, noise abatement, animal control--"

"So you really *are* a dogcatcher?"

"No, asshole, I'm not."

"Then you're a meter maid?"

"Screw you," Pilate said, laughing. "It pays some bills. All I have to do is be a calming presence and keep the county advised of what's happening until they get the sheriff's department back up to full strength."

"Okay, I get it. I just…well, I never expected to see you wearing a badge, 'specially after all that shit went down in Key West."

"Me neither."

"Can you see that Key West PD sergeant's face? What's his name? Tom something? If he found out you're wearin' a badge, he'd be the one with a heart problem."

"Well, let's not tell him, okay?" Pilate said before he took another sip.

"Fair enough," Taters agreed. "By the way, I ran into Buster the other day. Sends his regards."

"Nice. Send 'em back when you see him again."

"Will do. There goes the sun." Taters sighed heavily. "Pretty, but you're right. It could do with a little green flash."

"You feel okay? Need to go rest?"

"John…"

"Yeah?"

"Shut up and get me another beer, would ya?"

* * *

"Cordwainer called, twice," Kate called from the back door.

"Crap." Pilate sighed, flicked a bottle cap into the night, and slapped his hand on the makeshift bar. "What the hell does he want at this hour?"

"He swears he's going to kill Mrs. Drum's dog if you don't get over there and put a muzzle on it."

"Tell him to screw off," Pilate said.

Taters snickered.

"I'm not your dispatcher. Sorry to interrupt you boys' play date, but it's your job, and you need to do it," she scolded before the back door shut behind her.

Pilate sighed and shrugged. "Duty calls."

"Can I come with you?"

"After a long plane ride and three beers? Aren't you tired?"

"I gained an hour, remember? I like central time."

"All right. C'mon then."

"This will be so exciting, you actin' like a cop instead of just bragging about screwing one."

"And to think that I've actually missed you."

* * *

"I can't believe you don't even get a patrol car or a cool pickup," Taters said, turning on the heater in the Saab. "Brrr. Beer wore off. When did it get cold?"

"You're not used to nights in the sixties, are you?"

"No."

"There's a seat warmer. Push that button. Want a shawl too, sweetheart?"

Taters flipped Pilate the bird and gulped the last of his Modelo.

"Won't take long to get there," Pilate said.

"I should think not," Taters said. "This town is like my Johnson, about two feet long and six inches wide."

"Wow. Those meds are really screwing with your mind, man."

Pilate noticed in the dim light of the Saab interior that Taters looked tired and a little frail. He was missing something, Pilate decided. *Perhaps the fire he possessed as a charter captain in the Gulf died with his heart episode.*

"Stop making snap judgments," Simon said.

Pilate pulled up to the street by Harley Cordwainer's place.

"Nice. American Gothic," Taters said.

Pilate turned the engine and headlights off. "Listen."

Taters cocked his head, listening intently. "I don't hear anything."

"Exactly." Pilate opened his door.

Taters put his hand on his own door handle.

"Buddy, you'd better wait here."

"Oh please, Sheriff--"

"Constable."

"Close enough. I didn't come this far to sit in the car."

"You said it wasn't far to go in this two-foot town."

Taters opened his door and extended his right leg onto the street.

Pilate did the same. "Fine, but stay behind me." Pilate picked up his Maglite from the back seat and led the way up the small hill that became Cordwainer's driveway.

The old manse was large, one of the largest homes in Cross. It could have been a B&B, something like Cusack's Cross and Cork. It had a vaguely sinister, gothic look. Faint light bled from a pair of windows on the first floor, like the eyes of a wary predator.

Pilate looked to his west, taking notice of the warm lights of Mrs. Drum's ranch-style home. He listened again for sounds of her yappy dog, but he didn't hear one bark or whimper.

"I thought we were here on a noise complaint."

"We are," Pilate whispered. "This is such bullshit."

"Kinda gives you new respect for Policewoman Kay Rig--"

Pilate shot Taters a look, silently cutting him off.

Taters held up his hands in surrender, knowing he had overstepped by again mentioning Pilate's Key West lover, Officer Kay Righetti. Pilate had spent a lot of time and therapy trying to get over the guilt about their dalliance and the fact that he almost got her killed by pirates in the Gulf.

"Let's go." Pilate strode up the hill to Cordwainer's front door. He gently nudged Taters back two feet behind him, then straightened the badge pinned to his jacket and rang the doorbell.

A moment later, the heavy oak door opened, revealing a bespectacled Harley Cordwainer, wearing a tattered bathrobe, large black glasses in a style favored by Swifty Lazar, and comical fuzzy slippers, reminiscent of a certain Warner Brothers cartoon character, though Pilate couldn't place which one.

"Oh, look. It's the fascist harassment team." Cordwainer sneered and stepped out on the porch, pulling the door shut behind him. "Who's this?"

"He's uh…well, a deputy."

"Deputy? They have a deputy constable now? What the fuck are my tax dollars going to?"

Taters snickered at the old professor.

"Something amusing you, pawn shop?" Cordwainer said, his eyes magnified by the cartoonish glasses.

"More than you know," Taters said.

"Zip it, Deputy," Pilate said over his shoulder to Taters.

"Yes, sir," Taters said, his voice quivering as he stifled another snicker.

"Harley?"

"The word your miniscule mind seeks is 'professor'."

"Professor, why are we talking?"

"Because that yappy dog next door is disturbing my peace…again," Cordwainer said. "I told your grouchy-ass wife that on the phone."

"Well, I don't hear anything," Pilate said.

"You would have if you'd have come an hour ago," he said. "Old lady Drum had that thing tied to a rope in her back yard, and it wouldn't shut the fuck up."

Pilate made a show of looking at his watch. "Professor, it is now nine thirty. The dog is inside, and all is quiet, so we have no business here." He turned on his heels, stopped, and looked back. "Goodnight…and from now on, might I remind you that I will respond to noise complaints only after ten p.m. on weekdays and after eleven thirty on Saturdays. Understood?"

"Does that include your deputy?"

"Him too."

"I warn you, Sheriff--"

"Constable."

"Close enough," Taters said.

"If that dog barks one minute after ten…or after eleven thirty on Saturday, I will--and I repeat, I will--take care of it."

"And I presume that means you'll call me?"

"A whole damn lotta good that seems to do, Constable," Cordwainer said, slipping back inside his home. With only his head poking out, he said, "Listen here, you rent-a-cop, wannabe-hack. I'm trying to finish my magnum opus, and I will not be thrown off track by the ridiculous barking of that supercilious old woman's cacophonous canine."

The magnum opus was also known as his "precious." For the past decade, Cordwainer had told anyone who would listen, in a voice far creepier than Sméagol's: "My precious will reinstall me into the pantheon of the great birds of the galaxy." Most doubted Cordwainer's personal demons would allow him to finish it. Mrs. Drum's dog was yet another convenient excuse, a diversion, especially now that his fifth wife had taken a plane back to California.

Pilate nodded. "Just let me take care of the dog. Call me, and don't do anything rash."

"You could just buy some noise-canceling headphones," Taters added.

"Impertinent swine. I will sue you into oblivion!" Cordwainer threatened, then slammed his door.

Pilate looked up into the brilliant, starry sky. "Thanks, Deputy. I really appreciate the backup."

Chapter Fourteen

The pleasant smell of Kate's egg-free eggs and turkey bacon were deceptive to Taters's taste buds. When he bit into the ersatz bacon, Taters made the same face he would have made had she served him a steaming plate of packing material.

Peter Pilate giggled in his highchair.

"Little smartass," Taters muttered, smiling. He shrugged. "Hey, turkey bacon is better than none at all, I guess, which is what I'd get at home,"

"There ya go," Pilate said. "Stay positive, Gramps."

"Like son, like father, apparently," Taters grumbled, again taking on a forced scowl.

"So...what do you little boys have planned today?" Kate asked, sliding a half-piece of buttered toast onto Kara's plate.

"As little as possible," Pilate said.

"What about work?"

"I have a cell phone, as well as a radio in the car," Pilate said. "We're just gonna hang out. Right, T?"

Taters nodded, chewing the turkey bacon. "Yeah, your husband promised to take me on the grand tour. After we kill that ten minutes, I figure we'll go fishing."

Kate smiled. "Not a bad idea. You can use Grif's tackle and poles if you want. He left a couple here. The pond would be great."

"Pond? What about the river?"

"River moves pretty fast," Pilate said, cocking his head and averting Taters's gaze.

"Um, okay. Whatever," Taters said.

"Kara, hurry up. You're gonna be late, honey," Kate said. She looked at Pilate. "Can you drop her off?"

"You bet. Taters and Toot."

"I'm not a toot, Dad!"

* * *

Pilate wheeled through the streets of Cross. Orange, yellow, and brown drifted down on the Saab.

"Damn. I haven't seen leaves like this since I lived in...well, since I was a kid, I guess."

"Pretty, isn't it?" Pilate said.

"I like it. Miss Prince and Mrs. Molloy let us play in the piles of leaves at recess," Kara piped up from the back seat.

"Cool. I like diving into a pile of leaves every now and then myself," Pilate said.

"Yeah, but you get all pissed off when you have to rake them up again," Simon said. *"Don't be so pretentious."*

Stopping at Live Oak and Tenth Street, Pilate eyed the humble but pristinely kept home of Gary Rich. Not one leaf was in his yard, despite a massive, century-old oak that dominated the grounds.

"John..."

"Huh?"

"It's a four-way stop in a one-horse town. I suspect you can go...or do you need to fire a handgun in the air and count to a hundred?"

"Yeah, yeah." Pilate pressed the gas pedal. "Just admiring that yard."

Taters looked behind them. "Whoa. Those folks must have nothing to do but rake all day. The yard across the street looks like it's six inches deep in leaves."

"Yeah, some people have different priorities."

The trio soon arrived at the elementary school.

Abbey Prince stood there, with her hands on her hips, welcoming students. Her face brightened when Pilate pulled up. "Hello, John!"

"Hi, Abbey," Pilate said, getting out and helping Kara exit the back seat.

"Good morning, Miss Kara," Abbey said.

"Good morning, Miss Prince," Kara answered. She turned to the door. "This is Mr. Potatoes."

Taters and Pilate burst into fits of laughter.

Abbey's face was a mix of bemusement and confusion.

"Taters," Pilate corrected. "Abbey, this is my pal from Key West, Taters Malley."

"Nice to meet you," Abbey said. "You're the boat captain?"

Taters opened the door and made a slight bow, then stood up straight and threw his shoulders back. "Captain? Well, I s'pose I am."

"I've heard about you," she said, smiling slyly.

"All lies, young lady," Taters said.

"Well, they were pretty nice things…"

"In that case, the truth and nothin' but the truth, young lady," he said.

The school bell rang.

"We'd better get inside. Come on, Kara. Nice to meet you, Mr. Malley. John."

The men nodded, smiling as Abbey and Kara walked inside.

"That's one sweet-looking teacher," Taters said, whistling low through his teeth.

"She is. Abbey was one of my students," Pilate said, twirling the car keys in his hand, watching her walk away. "She's good people."

"Wait. Is she the one who was hot for teacher?"

Pilate smiled.

"I'll take that as a yes," Taters said, climbing in the car. "Where to?"

"Let's have a look around town. I'll show you the sights."

"Sounds good."

"You still up for fishing after?"

"Hell yes, though I'm not sure I can eat freshwater fish after being in the Gulf so long. Might be too much of a shock to the ol' ticker."

"Shit, I'm not sure we can even catch freshwater fish. But hey, it's an excuse to have some Modelos."

"Yeah, there's that."

* * *

Pilate showed Taters the highlights, starting with the Cross College library. Pilate hadn't spent much time inside it since he was nearly murdered there by the librarian last year, and he didn't plan to today; standing outside would do.

"So this is where you had it out with that Crawling fella?"

"Krall," Pilate said, his voice low. "Derek Krall, and yes, this is where it happened," Pilate said, recalling his recent conversation with Parker Nemec.

The carillon went off, playing "If I Were A Rich Man."

Taters pointed up at the bell tower in the library. "And that's where you waited out the storm before you trudged through all that snow to get to a radio?"

Pilate nodded. "Seems so long ago."

"Hell, our little adventure on the high seas in the Gulf seems like ages ago to me," Taters said.

"Lotta water under the bridge."

"John Pilate? Hey!" Dean Felix said, walking from the library door to where the men stood.

"Hello, Dean," Pilate said. "Dean Don Felix, this is my friend, Taters Malley."

"Taters?" He extended a hand. "How do you do?"

"Just fine, thank you," Taters said, shaking the Dean's hand.

"New in town?"

"Just visiting," Taters answered. "Dean, is it?"

"Don." He chuckled. "Don the dean."

"Don, it's a pleasure."

"John was just showing me around the prettiest campus in Iowa," Taters said.

"Nebraska," Pilate said.

"Close en--"

"Yeah, we're pretty proud of our campus. It's an officially recognized arboretum site."

"Impressive," Taters said.

"Well, where you from, Mr., uh…Taters?"

"Malley. My last name's Malley. Taters is a nickname."

"Oh, I see. Well, welcome. What brings you here, to Nebraska, I mean?"

"Just visiting my old buddy," he said, elbowing Pilate in the ribs.

"We love John," Felix said, hitching his pants up on his hips; his belt needed help.

"Oh go on," Simon said. *"No, really. Go on, you annoying little man."*

"He really put Cross College on the map," Felix said, wiggling his eyebrows. "So, Mr. Malley, what do you do?"

"Taters is a charter boat captain, Don," Pilate said, irritation creeping in. "Don't worry. He's not a reporter."

Taters burst out laughing. "Far from it!"

All color flushed from Felix's face. "Am I that transparent?"

"Not at all," Pilate said, his voice dry as a Hawkeye Pierce martini.

"Well, again," the dean said, clearing his throat, "welcome, Taters."

Taters nodded and smiled.

"So, John, I hear you're the town constable now," Felix said.

"Yep. Only temporary, but I've got bills to pay."

"Well, I can't think of a better guy. Hey, maybe you can teach a section of criminal justice next semester." Felix laughed, a little too hard.

"You'll be lucky if he does," Taters said, matching the laugh with one of his own.

"Well played," Simon said.

"You're 100 percent right," Felix said. "Well, John," he said, turning back to Pilate, "could we talk about coordinating campus security with your efforts sometime?"

"Sure, Don," Pilate said. He wanted to add that he was only working the job for a few more months, but he saw no point. "Call my office tomorrow, and we'll set something up."

"You bet. Well, I'd better get to a meeting. Taters, it's been a pleasure."

"All mine," Taters said.

"John."

Pilate nodded as the man took his leave, hurrying up the sidewalk to the administration building.

"Now I see why that guy shot his dean in 1963," Taters said.

"Jeez, Taters. He's not that bad," Pilate said.

"Sorry. The guy just seems a little full of himself."

"He's a college dean."

"Got it. I just forgot how those guys in, uh…what do you call it? Anemia?"

"Academia?"

"Yeah, that."

"They're not all bad. Most are just pumped up on the prestige of being a big fish in a little pond."

"Then there are the ones who go psycho and try to kill you, like the former president here," Simon said.

"Gotcha."

Pilate looked across the oval, eyeing the bench where he'd first met former Cross College president, Jack Lindstrom. Pilate had driven in with a U-Haul and passed the time with a cigarette, waiting for the admin office to open. He carelessly tossed a butt on the ground, something Lindstrom observed and promptly upbraided him for doing. It went downhill from there.

"John, where to now? You okay?"

"Sorry," Pilate said, shrugging. "Lot of crap memories."

Taters cocked his head. "Tough for you here, isn't it?"

"It's not so bad."

"Bullshit. All things considered, the sightseeing trip to that cemetery on the hill is officially off the itinerary."

* * *

For the next hour, Pilate showed Taters some other sights: the greasy spoon, the VFW hall, the bank, the post office, and, finally, his office.

Taters wandered about the outer office, admiring the heavy shutters on the windows and front door, then the small jail cell. "Man, this is like something out of a John Wayne flick," Taters said. "You take the speakerphone off the desk and squint a little, and I feel like John T. Chance could walk in anytime."

"Ha. Never thought of that," Pilate said.

"You've got a jail. Can you arrest people?"

"Technically," Pilate said, "but then I'd have to be up here all night with them. That cell's mostly for show these days. Especially during my very brief administration."

"Ya never know," Taters said. "Hey, I've got an idea." He fished in his pocket and handed Pilate his phone, then walked into the cell. "Take my picture."

Pilate laughed. "Okay, but don't--"

Taters pulled the door closed.

"Close the door."

"What?"

"Taters, I don't have the keys on me. They're at home."

"You shittin' me?" Taters's face was a mask of confusion, annoyance, and a slight terror.

Pilate took the picture. "Gotcha."

"Damn you, John. Don't go pullin' practical jokes on a man with an alien heart. Now get me outta here."

Pilate unlocked the door. "Ready to go catch some fish?"

Before Taters could answer, a voice called from the front door, a female voice, shaky and trying hard to maintain composure: "Constable? Constable? Are you in there?"

"Yes, I'm here. What's up?" Pilate asked, tossing Taters his phone and rushing to the front office.

Standing in the front doorway was a middle-aged woman with brown hair, hollow eyes, and blood smeared on her blouse. "Constable, y-you have to hurry. It's Parker. I think he's…d-dying!"

Chapter Fifteen

Bursting out the door, Pilate, followed closely by Taters, ran ten feet, to a ridiculously large pickup, idling, its chrome nose smashed into one of the ionic bank pillars.

Pilate recognized Parker Nemec lying on the ground. The lower half of his body was in his Ford F-150, but the other half was hanging out of the truck cab, twitching on a grim halo of blood.

Pilate kept his eyes on Nemec and bellowed, "Call 911!" He crouched beside the man, looking for a wound. "Mr. Nemec? Parker?"

Nemec's eyes fluttered in recognition.

"Parker, what happened?"

The woman crumpled against the truck fender.

Taters took her arm. "You need to sit down, little lady," he said, guiding her away from the scene, over to a bench in front of the bank. "Where's your phone?"

Nemec muttered something unintelligible.

Pilate could barely hear him and rose up. He leaned over Nemec and turned the key. Before the banker fell out of the vehicle, he had somehow marshaled the strength to take the truck out of gear.

Pilate carefully pulled him from the truck cab and laid him on the street, then bent down over the bloodied body. "Parker, what happened?" He took the man's blood-speckled face in his hands and tried to make eye contact. He knew it was critical to get as much information as possible.

"Cold…" Nemec shuddered.

Pilate was no expert, but he knew that was a sign of shock and significant blood loss. "We'll get you fixed up, Parker. Just tell me what happened."

"Axe…me…" he muttered through chattering teeth.

"Ask you what? What happened?" Pilate felt Nemec's body shuddering violently beneath him.

"Axed me," he said.

"Asked you what? Parker, listen to me," Pilate spoke calmly in measured, comforting tones. "We have a call in to the paramedics. You're gonna be okay, but I need you to do two things for me. Can you?"

Nemec's eyes fluttered.

"Okay. One, understand that you are going to live, and try to breathe normally. Can you do that?" Pilate didn't wait for a response. "Two, tell me who hurt you."

"He axed me," Nemec said, each syllable clearly a herculean effort.

"What? What did he ask you? Who asked you?"

"This is turning into a sick game of who's-on-first," Simon said.

"In my…back," Nemec stammered.

Pilate gently placed Nemec's head on the ground. "Parker, I'm going to lift you up and have a look."

"No! Don't touch me. Hurts… Axed me, and…" Nemec stuttered, then blacked out.

"Shit." Pilate pulled Nemec gently on his side. Nemec's sport shirt was soaked with blood and had a massive tear in it. Pilate moved the shirt around and found a gash, about five inches long and an inch or so wide, almost horizontal, dead center between his shoulder blades.

"Looks like someone swung a baseball bat at him," Simon said.

"No, an axe," Pilate sighed, gently holding Nemec's body. "Somebody axed him all right."

Sirens flooded his ears.

"They're on the way," Taters said from behind Pilate.

Pilate nodded.

"Guess that fishing trip is off, huh?"

* * *

Burl Crites, the county paramedic, rolled up in his ambulance seconds later. "What we got, Sheriff?"

Pilate didn't think to correct him with his proper, less impressive title. "Stabbing, right up between his shoulder blades." He nodded his head at the gaping wound.

Crites knelt beside them and called over his shoulder, "Story, we need a pressure bandage…now!"

Pilate's watched as Story Sudik, an Explorer student EMT, smoothly dropped to the ground beside them with her medical kit. Such professionalism and maturity, which went well beyond her sixteen years, had earned her a commendation from the governor when former Sheriff Welliver was shot. She and Crites were first responders, and Story had played a role in saving the sheriff's life.

Pilate stood and thoughtlessly wiped his hands on his shirt.

"Burl, that look like an axe wound to you?"

Crites nodded. "Could be." His voice was level as he went about his work. "Sheriff, we're gonna stabilize him the best we can and get him to hospital. He's lost some blood, but I think he'll pull through if things go our way."

"I need to know who did this to him," Pilate said, watching Crites and Sudik working on Nemec.

"Understood," Crites said. "If he comes to and says anything, we'll take note. Story, get ready to move."

She nodded, glancing back at Pilate a second before returning to her work.

* * *

"Who'd want to give that guy the cherry tree treatment?" Taters asked, leaning on the doorjamb as Pilate washed up.

In his small office sink, Pilate scrubbed the blood off his hands. "I have an idea or two."

Taters handed him several paper towels. "What do you do now?"

"Where did you find paper towels?"

"Under that crummy sink. Old, though--Brawny looks like a teenager on the package. He can barely grow a proper mustache."

"Well, thanks. I gotta make a call to the county about it, and State Patrol will probably be here any minute now to take statements. How's Sally, at the bank?"

"Shook up." He shrugged. "She's okay, but that other gal, Stephanie… well, her husband showed up, and they're pulling it together."

"How about you?" Pilate asked, stepping out of the bathroom.

"What about me?"

Pilate nodded at Taters's chest.

"Ticker? Fine," he said, waving Pilate off. "Really."

"Okay. You want me to take you home? I'm gonna need to hang around here and--"

"I don't wanna tell you your business, John, but I'm a witness, too, so maybe I should loiter a while longer."

"Totally right," Pilate said.

He was interrupted by a familiar voice: "John? You here?"

"Yup. I'll be right out, Commissioner."

Jeremy Ryder's tan, leathery face looked close to ashen as he stood in the outer office. "Jesus, Pilate. You got blood all over you too."

"Not as bad as Parker Nemec," Pilate said.

Ryder looked past Pilate. "Who's this gentleman?"

"My friend, Taters Malley," Pilate said.

Ryder nodded. "Mr. Malley, are you from around here?"

"He's visiting from Florida. He was with me when all this went down," Pilate said. "He'll need to give a statement to the state police, I imagine."

Ryder nodded. "Hulsey just rolled up behind me. You guys can talk to him in a minute. First, tell me what happened."

Pilate recounted everything to an impassive Ryder, who leaned on Pilate's desk, his arms folded and his legs crossed at his ostrich boot-ensconced ankles.

"Mr. Malley, was that about the way you saw it too?"

Taters nodded. "Well, I only saw a bit of it. I took Sally inside and called paramedics. John saw way more."

"Okay, Mr. Malley. Please go on out and give your statement to the trooper, would ya?"

Taters nodded.

"Thanks," Ryder said. After Taters closed the glass door, Ryder dropped into Pilate's chair and sighed, his steely blue eyes unfocused.

Pilate fell heavily in the guest chair in front of the desk.

"An axe?" Ryder's eyes still tracked ethereal.

Pilate nodded.

"Well, that narrows it down to every swinging dick in the county," Ryder said bitterly.

Pilate glanced down at the bloodstains on his shirt. "I suppose so, but I might have an idea. I mean, I don't wanna wrongly accuse anyone, but—"

"Go on." Ryder's eyes snapped over to Pilate's.

"Well, I was over at the Tin Roof Rib Shack the other day, and a fella met me there with an axe in his hand."

Ryder's eyes widened. "Really? Who?"

"He called himself Mr. Tibbs."

"Clever. Black guy?"

Pilate nodded.

"One of Robie's crew." Ryder fished a toothpick from his shirt pocket and jabbed it in his slit of a mouth. "Otis."

"Well, if it was, I think we all know who that points back to," Pilate said.

"Shit yeah," Ryder said, "but why? I mean, Parker Nemec's a damn banker. Sure, bankers ain't terribly popular these days, but--"

"He came to see me a few days ago," Pilate chimed in. "It was kinda odd, and he seemed a little…shaken up. I wasn't sure what he wanted."

Ryder keened a moment. "Scared?"

"Who? Him or me?"

"Him. Was he scared?"

Pilate nodded. "Seemed like it, though I never met the man before, so I couldn't be sure."

"Hmm. Well, somebody musta put a scare in him, then put a little English on the ball for good measure," Ryder said.

"Whoever it was, they took a pretty good swing, for sure," Pilate said.

"We need to find out where Nemec was when he got sucker-punched with that axe," Ryder said. "Evidently, he was close to his ride and managed to get back here. I doubt he coulda gotten far with that wound before he passed out."

"Do you want me to look into it?"

"Shit, John, you're the town constable, not a detective, remember?" Ryder said, smirking. "But you do have a certain…native ability when it comes to these things, a good track record, of sorts."

"True." Pilate felt his guts clenching again.

"Still, this isn't your job, and whoever these guys are, they're playing hardball. It's not that you haven't seen your share of the rough stuff, but I'd rather you stay out of it for the sake of your family. Let's let the state boys handle it good and proper," Ryder said, drawing his thin frame to a standing position. "But keep your eyes and ears open." Ryder clapped a hand on Pilate's shoulder as he walked past.

"Will do."

"Thanks, John. Let's go tell Hulsey what you know."

"Okay."

"By the way, where'd you get those crappy boots? Look like something a damn Okie would wear."

Chapter Sixteen

Pilate pushed a Modelo Especial across the grain of the FrontDoor Backyard Bar to Taters, amidst the buzz of night bugs coming alive at sundown.

"You gonna have one or keep drinking that fancy shit?" Taters asked.

Pilate leaned on the other side of the makeshift bar, his eyes on the martini. "Today's distinctly a martini day, pal."

"No arguments there," Taters said, inhaling deeply and opening the Modelo.

Pilate was on his second drink and feeling every drop of it. "This place is cursed," Pilate said, looking away from Taters, out at the denuded fields behind them.

"Now, John…" Taters started.

"I'm serious. This place is cursed and has been since that freaking nut-job, Professor Bernard, blew away his bosses here in '63," Pilate said, then sipped more of his drink. "There are ghosts walking these streets, Taters, haunting that school, and they demand satisfaction."

"Ghosts? That's horse shit, and you know it."

Pilate smiled humorlessly, observing a gnat dying in his drink. "Maybe you're right. Maybe it isn't the town that's cursed."

"Exactly."

"Maybe it's me." Pilate drank the gnat.

"John, don't be so dramatic."

"You know how many people have died in this town since I got here?"

Taters nodded.

"And how many people died in Key West when I got there? How many people nearly died, including you?"

Taters chewed his lip a moment. "John, stop it."

Pilate reached for his martini shaker.

"Do you really think you need more of that stuff? It's already got you talkin' crazy, 'bout ghosts and curses and other such nonsense."

Pilate nodded.

"Okay. Well, do whatever you need to do," Taters said, then drank his beer. "I'm not one to call the kettle black."

"John!" Kate called from the back door.

"Yeah, babe?"

"You guys ready to call it a day yet?"

"In a few," Pilate said, barely concealing his irritation; he wanted to drink.

Kate nodded and closed the door.

"John..." Taters murmured, the mouth of his beer bottle an inch from his face.

"Yeah?"

"Bad things happen to good people every damn day. You're no special case."

Pilate stopped pouring the last drops of vodka, gin, and vermouth from the shaker into his glass and looked at Taters. "I know some ghosts who'd beg to differ."

* * *

Cusack carried wood from the pile, around to the large fire pit behind the bed-and-breakfast, then stacked it carefully for the night's blaze.

"Hallo, Cusack." An Irish accent dropped from the trees, breaking the silence and startling Cusack, who dropped his firewood. "Sorry to startle. Did you think it was himself, the Sluagh?"

"No, just a fookin' gowl," Cusack said, picking up the wood and arranging it.

"Ha! I'd still say you oughtta close your west-facin' windas," Jackie the Crow said, stepping from behind a massive oak, tendrils of smoke rising from his nostrils, billowing heavenward. He paused a moment and looked about him as he tapped the ashes from the cigarette in his gnarled hand. "You know, this Cross is a far cry from *da Cross* of our own."

Cusack nodded. "Leesiders wouldn't know what to make of it."

Both men paused in silence until Jackie flicked a bit of loose tobacco from his lip.

"There've been some...doin's."

"And it concerns my business?" Cusack said, keeping his eyes on the kindling.

"You could say that," Jackie said. "Somebody was due for the chop, and they surely got it."

"Must you always talk like you're smarter than ya are? Fool eegit. Just spit it out plain."

"Let's just say that an obstacle has been...cut down," Jackie said.

Marcy called from the wraparound porch.

"Better go now, Cusack," Jackie said. "You wouldn't want your classy wife ta see ya hanging with a Culchie chancer like me. Might let it slip to the five-oh."

Cusack shot him a look, raised a hand, and pointed a finger at Jackie. After a beat, he turned and wordlessly trudged back to the house.

Jackie snickered and slipped back into the woods; only a few puffs of smoke hung in the air to mark his presence.

* * *

Kate put a cup of coffee in front of Pilate as he sat at the kitchen table, holding Peter in the crook of his right arm. Pilate's mug featured a *Star Trek*-style red shirt and the phrase, "He's dead, Jim."

"How's your head?"

"Fine."

She nodded. "Okay. You need to take Kara to school in twenty," she said. "I'm dropping Peter off at daycare before my eight thirty."

"Okay, babe."

Kate put her hair in a loose bun, gathered her school bag, and slung her purse over her shoulder.

Pilate looked at Peter's face. His downy blond hair and dark eyes captivated Pilate's attention. He felt a strange lump in his throat, and a tear formed in his right eye. "Kate, I, uh…" he started, then stopped to clear his throat.

"Hmm?"

"I love this little guy so much," he said. "I mean, I hate to even send him off to daycare. Not all the time, but every now and then. I just hate having to let him go."

Kate smiled. "Honey, like I told you before, if you didn't feel that way at least once in a while, I'd say you were a sucky dad." She leaned over and kissed Pilate's forehead, reaching for their son. "C'mon, baby," she cooed.

Pilate kissed Peter's soft cheek. "Bye, pal," he whispered, letting his wife take the baby from his arms.

Kate took Peter's little arm and gently made it wave at Pilate. "Say bye to Daddy. Bye-bye, Daddy!"

Pilate rose to his feet and took them both in his arms and held them tight.

After a moment, Kate pulled back. "John?"

"I'm fine."

"After what you saw yesterday…well, we're okay, right?"

"Right."

She kissed him and scooped up her car keys. "Have a good day with Taters. Don't make Kara late."

"Okay," he said, wiping the tear away and watching as his son waved from his mother's shoulder. "Bye, kiddo."

* * *

Taters, donning a Hobie t-shirt and Bermuda shorts, ambled downstairs as Pilate helped Kara with her jacket and her *Dora the Explorer* backpack.

"Off to school, little lady?" Taters asked.

"Uh-huh," she said. "It's show-and-tell day."

"Oh shit," Pilate said. "I mean…shoot. What are you taking, honey?"

Kara twisted her lips in a grimace. "Um, something."

"What, baby?" Pilate asked. "We have to hurry, or we'll be late."

Kara looked at her feet. "It's supposed to be something Daddy or Mommy uses for work."

Pilate smiled. "So who did you pick, Mommy or Daddy?"

"Daddy."

"Okay. Great. I don't see a typewriter in that backpack, Kara, so what did you pick?"

"A martini shaker?" Taters said.

Pilate glared at him, then smiled. "Nice. There's coffee in the kitchen."

"What's a typewriter?"

"Never mind. Kara, we need to hurry. What did you pick?" Pilate considered the grief he caught from Kate the last time he forgot show-and-tell.

Kara took off her backpack and dug around in it for a second, then seized something and announced, "This!" In her hand was a cylindrical, shiny object, a little less than an inch long.

Pilate snatched it from her hand. "Where did you get this? Kara Jane, answer me now."

Kara blanched. "It was behind the table, beside your bed," she said, her lip protruding.

"Kara, do you know what this is?" Pilate asked, kneeling beside her.

"Yes. It's part of your gun. You use it at work."

Pilate's heart sank. He took a deep breath and exhaled. He took Kara by her shoulders. "Honey, this is a bullet. If it's in a gun, it can hurt people. I don't ever, ever want you to touch guns or bullets." Pilate cursed himself, remembering that he'd dropped a box of cartridges a few days earlier, as he locked his pistol in the safe. He thought he had found them all, but he obviously hadn't.

"Am I in trouble?" Kara's eyes moistened.

"No. Just please remember that guns and bullets are not toys, and you must never touch them, okay?"

"Okay, but it is part of your job, Daddy."

Pilate's head began to swim, and it wasn't just the hangover. "Kara, honey, listen. Guns and bullets are not for my job. Making sure people follow the law is my job, and it's not even a real job for me. I mean, I'm not really a policeman. I'm just helping the sheriff."

"Daddy, you said your job is to keep me safe."

Pilate felt a lump forming in his throat. "That's right," he said, giving her a gentle hug. "That's right, but Kara, sweetie, Daddy's also a teacher and a writer. You could take a pencil or a book." Pilate stopped abruptly, suddenly thinking better about sending a copy of his book about murders in Cross Township with a seven-year-old. The dustcover alone would give kids nightmares.

Taters leaned out of the kitchen door, drinking from Pilate's mug. "Better hurry, John. School bell's gonna ring."

Pilate nodded quickly.

"Daddy, I have to take something, or I'll be the only one--"

"Okay, Kara. Calm down." Pilate looked around the room. "Here," he said. "Take this." He walked over to small table by the door, where he kept his wallet and keys.

"Wow!" Kara said.

"Beats a stupid bullet, huh?"

"Yes! Nobody will have anything like this." She danced around the room with the shiny brass object in her hand.

"You are now an official honorary deputy constable for the day." Pilate smiled. "Just don't lose it, okay? The commissioner will be pissed…er, mad if I lose it."

"But, Daddy, how will you work without your badge?" Kara said, suddenly thoughtful. "How will the bad guys know who to obey?"

"The same way I work without a gun," he said. "I just…make it so."

Taters smiled and nodded, drinking coffee and winking at Kara.

"Say goodbye to Uncle Taters," Pilate said, opening the front door.

As Kara hugged Taters goodbye, he caught a reflection of himself in the mirror hanging by the door. Behind him was Simon, smirking, with his arms folded.

"So, you're not a writer or teacher after all. You're a cop, without a badge or a gun."

Pilate looked away. "Let's go, little toot," he said.

"I am not a little toot! You said I'm a deputy today!" Kara said, holding the badge in front of her as she walked, as if it was a guiding star. "Boy, this is heavy."

"Tell me about it," Pilate said.

* * *

Due to the bullet fiasco, Pilate and Kara ran late and missed the bell.

"C'mon, Kara," he said, pulling her by the hand.

"Okay," she said, still clutching his constable badge.

The school door was locked, so Pilate cupped his hands around his eyes and peered in. Spying a familiar shape, he knocked.

Abbey Prince opened the door. "Good morning! Tardy, tardy, Kara Jane." she smiled. "Did Daddy drive too slowly?"

Kara held up the badge. "He's the police. He's allowed to be tardy."

Abbey's eyes widened as she looked at the badge. "Well, that's true." She looked at Pilate with an are-you-aware-she-has-that expression.

He nodded. "Show-and-tell," he said.

"Oh, right," Abbey said. "Something from your parent's work, right? I guess your book was out of the question."

"Definitely," Pilate said.

"I'll take her to class, John," she said. Abbey was wearing a white blouse, blue skirt, and low heels. Her blonde hair was in a ponytail, not quite a match with her outfit. She was also sans makeup, a face a bit less elegant than her clothing.

"Looks like she was running a tad late herself today," Simon said.

"Okay. Thanks, Abbey. We'll see you later," he said.

Kara waved at Pilate. "Bye, Sheriff Daddy!"

"Sheriff Daddy?"

"Shut up, Simon," he muttered, smiling and waving.

Chapter Seventeen

Pilate stopped at the convenience store to gas up the Saab and get another cup of coffee.

"Mornin', Sheriff," said Tracey, the pimply, plump clerk behind the counter, not looking up from her newspaper.

"Constable," he said as he walked by, taking note of glazed donuts on the counter. Pilate never ate donuts, the harbingers of far too many empty calories, and he had to wonder if the old cliché was true and the badge was getting the best of him.

But today might be a donut day.

He poured a half-cup of coffee from the red-handled carafe, then topped it with decaf from the carafe with the green handle. "I'm gonna fill up the car too," he said.

"Okay," Tracey said. "On the county?"

"No. I'll pay for it," he said.

She shrugged as he placed his coffee on the counter. "Well, the coffee's on the county."

"Why?"

"The law drinks free," she said, glancing up at him sideways, as if he was stupid for not knowing that already.

"Oh, well…" Pilate thought for a second about turning it down but realized it was the way things worked, and sixty-seven cents wasn't worth arguing about anyway. "In that case, I'll take a donut too."

"Donuts are fifty cents."

"Not on the county?"

She didn't look up. "Coffee's on the county. Donuts ain't."

"Of course." Pilate dropped two quarters on the counter.

As he fed the Saab, he also fed himself, munching on the donut and sipping his coffee.

"Oh my God," Simon said. *"You really are a cop. Really, what's more ubiquitous in law enforcement than the patrolman's diet? Who needs a badge or a gun? You have coffee and a donut."*

Pilate swallowed the bite of donut and dropped the rest in the trash.

* * *

Gary Rich paced in front of the constable's office, his hands thrust deep in the pockets of his green Army jacket, eyeing the massive dent Parker Nemec's truck had left in the bank pillar next door.

"Great," Simon said as Pilate parked the Saab, sighing.

Pilate barely had one leg out of the car before Rich was upon him, his hands now on his waist.

"Constable, we have a real problem here," the self-proclaimed neighborhood watchman said, a touch of spittle on his lips.

"Oh? And good morning to you, too, Captain," Pilate said, exiting and closing the car door.

"Constable," he started, "are you even partially aware of what is happening in this town you're sworn to protect?"

"I'm sure I don't know everything," Pilate said, finding the key to his office on his key ring as he walked to the door, "but I bet you're ready to shed some light on it for me."

Pointing at the ruined pillar, Rich continued. "A man nearly died here yesterday. He was assaulted."

"Yes, I know. I was there."

Rich stopped a second and looked down and to his right, as if receiving a signal from some secret satellite. "And you did nothing to stop it!"

"Stop it? How could I have stopped it?" Pilate said, turning the key in the door lock.

"It's your job!"

Pilate wheeled and faced Rich. "Mr. Rich," he started, dropping the "captain" pointedly, "the only way I could have stopped it would have been to invent a time machine and follow Mr. Nemec around all day yesterday."

"Well, that's just silly."

"And so is your premise," Pilate growled.

"My, my--"

"The idea that a small-town constable is supposed to be everywhere anytime to prevent crime is a stup..." Pilate paused, trying to think of something more professional to say. "It is an unrealistic premise. I do the best I can."

"If a prominent member of our town can be attacked by a machete,--"

"Machete?"

Rich rolled on. "In broad daylight too! That indicates that the criminal element here does not fear your authority."

"Fear my authority? Just where the hell do you think we live? Russia?"

"This would never have happened under Sheriffs Welliver or Scovill," he sputtered.

"Mr. Rich, several people were murdered or nearly murdered during that time, including both of those sheriffs...and me!"

Rich pointed a stubby finger at Pilate. "Then you, of all people, should know better. You *will* be held accountable."

"For what specifically? The attack on Parker Nemec or the beer cans littering the streets? Or is it the dog shit on Mrs. Drum's lawn?"

"Mocking me will not help the situation sir," Rich said, trying to pass into the office, only to be barred by Pilate's arm.

"Oh, I disagree," Simon said.

"Mr. Rich, I'm working with the state police, the county leadership, and consulting with my entire unabridged Ellery Queen collection to figure out all this stuff--all for $1,013 a month."

"Plus mileage," Simon added.

"It's not good enough. Look at you," he said, glaring at Pilate, a sneer forming. "You don't even wear a gun, and where's your badge? You don't take this seriously. You're gonna get a wake-up call. Man, you better be ready." Rich's voice was quieter, almost solemn, his eyes downcast. "Some people can see evildoers from the get-go. You can't."

"Wait just a minute," Pilate said, taking a step closer to Rich.

Rich backed away. "I hope you're up to the task." He turned away and climbed on a beat-up ten-speed bike.

"Is that some sort of threat?" Pilate called after him.

"Beware Gary Rich's wrath," Simon said. *"I think he was in REO Speedwagon."*

Pilate stood a moment, watching the strange man pedal away, his knees pumping vigorously, his eyes forward. After a while, he shook his head and turned back to his office, his eye catching the damaged bank façade.

The office phone rang, breaking his train of thought.

"Constable, uh…?"

"Are you sure?" Ryder said.

"Sorry. Yeah, I'm sure. I just had a weird moment."

"That little town is full of weird moments," Ryder said with a snort.

"Don't you dare try to pin this town on me, Boss."

"Suit yourself." Ryder cleared his throat. "Anyway, Nemec woke up. Wanna head over to the hospital with me to question him? Petersen from state police will be there at ten."

"Sure," Pilate said. "Have we had a guard on him?"

"No, though we probably should have," Ryder said. "Low manpower's a bitch."

"Maybe our neighborhood watch should be called in," Pilate said.

"Oh shit, like that nut Gary Rich? Hell no. He'd probably try to waterboard somebody for taking Nemec's vitals."

"Speaking of him, what's his story?"

"Rich?" Ryder sighed. "He's the character you sensitive types would describe as having issues. His dad owned a farm a couple counties over. He was a John Bircher with a capital J and capital B, you know, one of those get-us-outta-the-U.N. bullshitters and all that new world order shit."

"I see."

"Anyway, the wife left him about ten years ago, and the old man died in a combine accident last year. Young Gary bought a house in Cross with the estate he inherited. What's up though? Is he botherin' ya?"

"He's been in here a couple times, telling me about all the evildoers."

"Yeah, well, he's mostly harmless," Ryder said. "See ya in a few."

"Mostly?" Simon said. *"How reassuring."*

* * *

Pilate dialed his home phone number.

"Hello?" Taters said.

"Hey, man, how you doing?"

"Fair to midland." He coughed. "And yourself?"

"Same," Pilate said. "Hey, look, sorry I got a little down last night."

"No explanation or apology necessary, man. We've seen too much shit together to start that," he said, chuckling softly.

"Thanks. You eat yet?"

"Had some toast and some of your wife's alleged bacon."

"Sorry about that too. Listen, I'm heading over to the hospital. That fella with the bad back is awake, and we're gonna question him, so I don't know when I'll be done."

"Gonna axe him some questions, huh?"

"Very punny."

"Can I come along?"

"I guess, but it's an official police thing, so you can't come in the room," Pilate said.

"I just figured we could grab some lunch after, maybe someplace that sells burgers or other health food."

"Sounds good. The questioning shouldn't take too long."

"Okay. Well, I'll get dressed and be ready for ya," Taters said.

"Gimme about twenty, and I'll pick you up."

Next, Pilate dialed Kate's office and got her voicemail. "Hey, sweetness, it's me. Just an update. Dropped Kara at school, then I had to deal with that nut from the neighborhood watch. Got a call from Ryder. Nemec's awake. Going to go question him, then take Taters to lunch. Hope you're having a great day. Kiss the little guy for me when you see him at lunchtime. Love you."

Pilate hung up, then groaned as he stretched and popped his neck and back. He looked around the dusty office, wondering what law enforcement officers in generations past would think of him.

"That you're an idiot," Simon said.

Pilate walked to the door, fishing in his pocket for his keys. A small key with a blue paint mark on it, the one for his desk, stopped him cold. Pilate loosed a heavy, defeated sigh and walked back to his desk.

He unlocked the center drawer, removed the pistol Ryder had issued him, and loaded the chamber with eight bullets. Slipping it back in the clip-on holster, he tucked it under his arm and left.

* * *

"I-I don't remember," Parker Nemec said, pale and miserable in his hospital bed, a pillow propping him up on his right side, so as not to stress his back injury.

Detective Petersen from the state police stood closest to him, talking and occasionally checking a small recorder to make sure it captured the interview.

Jeremy Ryder stood in the corner, ever the laconic cowboy, leaning with one boot against the wall, his arms folded.

Pilate stood in the other corner of the tiny room, feeling distinctly extraneous.

"You really have no idea what you're doing," Simon insultingly observed.

Pilate didn't disagree with his doppelganger.

"You don't remember who hit you?"

Nemec's eyelids fluttered. "Not just that. I-I don't remember what happened." He was clearly on some decent pain meds.

"Let's step back." Petersen's tone was calm and patient, as if he was really just trying to be helpful.

Pilate had only met him once in person, but they had spoken often by phone. In fact, that one time they met, Petersen was interviewing Pilate about his role in the events the led to the murders at Cross College. Pilate observed that Petersen, a plain-clothes officer, looked as if he'd lost quite a bit of weight.

"Do you remember where you were when this happened?"

Nemec nodded slightly. "I was out by the Tin Roof, going to get some ribs."

That's more like it, Pilate thought.

"Okay. So you were out at the Tin Roof or near it?" Petersen asked.

"Well, I was parked there, going in," Nemec said dully.

"And that was around lunchtime?"

Nemec nodded again.

"Were there other people there?"

"Inside?" Nemec said. "I guess."

"But you were outside?"

"Yeah, out back."

"Why?"

Nemec blanched and looked behind Petersen, to the window on the east side of the room.

"Mr. Nemec?" Petersen said.

Ryder looked down at the one boot planted on the floor.

"I may be mistaken," Nemec said, barely a whisper.

Petersen moved the recorder closer to Nemec on the portable hospital table. "Mistaken? How?"

"I really don't know if I should say anything. I'm really tired, and those pills made me--"

"Mr. Nemec, we need to know what happened."

Nemec's eyes tracked back to Petersen. "Did you see that pretty lady outside the room? She's my wife, Wendy. I say anything to you, and something happens to her and me. I don't care about me, but Wendy's my whole world."

"We will protect both of you," Petersen said assuredly.

Nemec smiled weakly. "With what? Him?" He gestured at Pilate. "No offense, Constable, but you don't know what you're doing. You don't even want the job. Hell, even Opie's dad wore a damn badge."

Pilate made an exasperated face as Petersen scanned his chest for the missing lawman's identification.

Ryder cleared his throat noisily. From beneath his cowboy hat, his gaze still pointed at the floor, Ryder intoned, "We can move you both out of town. Detective Petersen can put you in protective custody."

Petersen looked at Ryder, his face barely masking his irritation. "What Commissioner Ryder means is that we can take steps to--"

"I want my lawyer and a guard, or I don't say another word."

"Is there someplace you and your wife can go--"

Pilate offered, "I know a place in Florida. Nobody'd know to look there."

Ryder looked up, eyeing Petersen and Pilate a second. He then looked back at Petersen and shrugged.

Nemec scanned all three faces. "Protective custody out of state? In Florida, for Wendy and me?"

Petersen took the ball and ran with it. "We could make that happen, but first, you have to tell us what happened and why."

"I wanna talk to Wendy and my lawyer first."

"No problem, Mr. Nemec," Petersen said. "Let's get Wendy in here, and she can call your attorney. We'll be back tomorrow. Sound good?"

Nemec nodded.

"But Parker," Ryder drawled, "make no mistake. We aren't just gonna drop the ball on this. We know there are no crazed axe murderers on the loose. We need to know what happened and why somebody was that pissed at you. If you decide not to cooperate, you'll spend some time in the hoosegow."

"Hoosegow? People really say that?" Simon said.

Nemec nodded, looking out the window again, and his hands began to tremble.

* * *

"I sure hope your office has the money to fly them on a Florida vacation, John," Petersen said in the small hospital chapel.

Ryder leaned on a pew, his arms folded. "It may be the only way we can get him to finger Thurman."

"Thurman?" Pilate said. "I figured it was one of Robie's guys."

"Robie and his guys don't take an impromptu shit without permission from Hilmer Thurman," Ryder said.

"But wouldn't an impromptu shit be one that would necessarily go without permission?" Simon inquired in Pilate's skull.

"Yes, John, we know Thurman's the new crime lord around here. That comes as no surprise. We have some suspicions that he's got designs on controlling the bank and perhaps acquiring a little more property."

"Like what?"

"Mostek's grocery, for one thing," Ryder said.

"Wait," Pilate said. "You think he'd kill a guy over a crummy little general store?"

Ryder nodded. "It's not just the store. It's the family that owns it. Ever since Perry Mostek disappeared after shooting Sheriff Welliver, we've had our suspicions that Hilmer Thurman was behind the whole mess. I think Parker Nemec is a wrinkle in Thurman's plans. He musta gotten cute with Hilmer and got an axe in the back for his trouble."

"But why would Thurman risk his little empire for this one deal?"

Petersen put a hand on Pilate's shoulder. "John, we're just spit-ballin' here, but we know Hilmer Thurman hates loose ends, and there's a rival bidding on that property. Maybe he was trying to convince the banker to sway the deal his way to freeze out the other buyer."

"Who's the other buyer?"

"You know that Scottish innkeeper, over at the B&B?" Petersen said.

"Yeah, but he's Irish actually." Pilate looked at Ryder, who again shrugged. "He wants the store?"

"Apparently," Petersen said. "According to records, he put a bid in, one that puts the property in play and will raise Thurman's price a bit."

"By how much?" Pilate said, exasperated. "A few thousand is hardly a reason to put an axe in a man's back. I mean, c'mon. I know Hilmer Thurman. He's a lot of things, but irrational isn't one of them."

"Well, aside from that, we have no other motive for a fella under Thurman's thumb to light out after Parker Nemec," Ryder said.

"There's gotta be more to this than meets the eye," Pilate said.

"Usually is," Petersen said, "but I'll be damned if I've got any reasonable ideas."

Pilate looked at Ryder, who kept his head dipped low, eyes obscured by his hat, even in the ersatz holiness of the hospital chapel. "Commissioner?"

Ryder looked up at the men, shrugging again. "Yeah, it doesn't make any sense. Looks like we've got a legit mystery here, fellas. Better call Scooby Doo."

Chapter Eighteen

"John, this is hardly what I'd call a decent lunch," Taters complained. "Hospital food?" All the same, Taters immediately dug in to the hamburger and side salad as if he hadn't eaten in days.

Pilate nodded. "At least it's meat. Sorry. Just got a lot going on today."

"Mm-hmm," Taters said, piling a few pieces of spinach and lettuce on his burger, then biting into it.

"Why would anybody go to such lengths over a damn real estate deal?"

Taters chewed a moment, then pointed at Pilate with his index finger. "Wasn't that the very reason your old pals Jack Lindstrom and Ollie Olafson went to war?"

Pilate looked at Taters. "Well, ultimately, yeah. I mean, there were some other issues at play, but Jack got involved because he wanted the land from the old Bartley place for his Cross College expansion plans. He also wanted to give Ollie the big eff-you."

Taters nodded. "So what you're saying is that it was really two guys trying to establish who was running things in this one-horse, no-beach town."

"He's smarter than he looks," Simon said.

Pilate nodded. "Yeah, but I don't… I mean, the Bartley deal was worth millions. The Mostek store is barely worth a couple hundred grand at best."

"Again," Taters said, around a mouthful of burger, "it may be about toeing the line, about this Thurman guy establishing who's in charge now."

Pilate snatched a piece of hard-boiled egg from his salad. "Okay, but let's think on this for a minute. If Thurman was mad about the deal getting pricier, why would he hurt the banker? Why not try to intimidate Cusack? He's the competing bidder."

Taters made an I've-got-no-idea face.

"Exactly."

Taters wiped his mouth with a paper napkin, then looked over Pilate's head, apparently lost in thought.

"What?"

Taters's eye took on a gleam Pilate had not seen since he'd last hung out with Taters in Key West. "Bigfoot."

"Huh?" Pilate said, putting his fork down.

"Remember the mystery submarine we found? The bigfoot?"

Pilate nodded. The pair had found, in the waters of the Gulf of Mexico, a small submarine commonly used for smuggling drugs, known as a Bigfoot because of the rarity of a sighting. They never knew what was in it, and the Department of Homeland Security forbade them from discussing it, under threats of bankruptcy and imprisonment.

"How can I forget, even though I'm supposed to?"

"Well, what if there's something in the Mostek place we don't know about? Somethin' this Thurman desperately wants access to?"

Pilate looked at Taters a moment. "A submarine?"

"Ha! Not necessarily, but something of value may be submerged under that storefront. You probably oughtta take a good, long look at it."

"Hmm. Not a bad idea, Taters," Pilate said. "Finish up your food, and we'll head over to the library."

"What? No fishing?"

"We'll be fishing all right."

* * *

As they started to leave the hospital parking lot, Pilate's cell phone rang.

"John? No dice on Nemec hitting the beach," Petersen said. "Just not in the budget, and frankly, I think if we sweat him a bit by reminding him that he's vulnerable, he'll talk anyway."

"Fine," Pilate said. "It was a dumb idea anyway, I guess."

"No, it had merit. Just wasn't...optimal," Petersen said.

"Hey, why do you think Thurman is so eager to get his hot little hands on that property?"

"Like I told you, John, I think he's swinging his dick around. Nemec got outta line and let Cusack get involved."

"Pretty thin, don't you think?"

Petersen sighed. "John, I don't know. Honestly, I'm working two homicides right now, and there's not a lot I can do about Parker Nemec until things change."

"Change how? Like him getting killed?"

"No, like him telling us what he knows."

"Okay. I hear ya. One last thing. Do you think there could be something to the actual Mostek store location?"

"What do you mean? Because it's the only grocery store in Cross? Yeah, that makes it valuable, especially considering that Piggly Wiggly and Safeway aren't exactly in a hurry to move one of their franchises in. It's a monopoly for the taking."

"I just mean the store location. Maybe there's...something else," Pilate said.

"Like what, the answer to the mystery of Oak Island? Al Capone's vault?" Petersen laughed.

"I don't know," Pilate said. "Maybe there's something in there we missed, something that lies beneath."

"Spooky stuff there, John. Well," Petersen said, sighing, "I gotta go, but you're the constable. Get a warrant and go take a look around if you think you'll find anything."

"Can I do that?"

"I actually don't know. There aren't many constables in Nebraska, so I'm not real up on the limits of your authority. Ask Ryder. I gotta go though. Be careful, Geraldo."

Click.

"He thinks I'm an idiot," Pilate said, putting his cell away.

"Screw 'im," Taters said.

Pilate took his cell phone out again and dialed the Cross College library. He spoke a few moments, then hung up. "Just like I thought."

"What?"

"The records on the Mostek place aren't housed there. The new librarian there said there used to be a substantial file, but it's gone missing," Pilate said, tucking his cell phone away. "Probably right around the time Parker Nemec started his so-called research."

"Well," Taters said, "I say we should go have a look at county."

"Good idea."

* * *

At the county records office, they found the plans for what became Mostek's store. It was originally a private residence. After an hour or so of digging around, with the help of a matronly, colorless records clerk named Patricia, they discovered that the town's first general store was built two doors down the same year, in 1897, on a plot of land that was a blacksmith's shop during the time when Cross was a mere camp on the river. That general store burned to the ground under mysterious circumstances a few years later.

"That's interesting," Taters mused. "Pretty damn big for a private residence."

"Yeah, that explains the architecture. It has a turret room above the main floor, and if it was built in the area plotted to be Main Street, I imagine there was some money involved."

Taters whistled low through his teeth. "Says here," he said, pointing, "that the house was built by one Thor Hilmer."

"What? Wait a second," Pilate said, drawing the plans closer and peering at the small print. "Hilmer. Thor Hilmer. I wonder if he's any relation to Hilmer Thurman?"

Patricia coughed and cleared her throat. "Sheriff…"

"Constable," Pilate said, not looking up.

"Constable, those plans were pulled recently. You didn't hear it from me, but they were pulled right about the time Ollie Olafson, um…well, you know."

Pilate looked at her. "About the time he died?"

She nodded.

"Who pulled the plans?"

Patricia adjusted her glasses and looked around the small, dusty records room conspiratorially. "A big guy named Tom. He was polite, but he looked like a truck driver. I'd never seen him before, and it just seemed odd that he would pull those plans, especially right after the mayor died and all."

Pilate nodded. "That is quite a coincidence."

Taters rolled his eyes. "Yeah, quite the co-inky-dink."

* * *

The pair said nothing until they got back in the Saab.

"So, what do you think, *kemosabe*?"

"Not sure, Sancho. I'd say there's definitely some Hilmer Thurman in this mix. Thurman's right-hand man is a fat guy named Tom."

"Well shit! There you go," Taters said, smacking one hand into the palm of the other.

Pilate breathed in deeply. "Let's think about this logically. Thurman's cousin Ollie, who runs Cross Township, dies." Pilate looked down a moment, shaking off the memory of the gunplay that led to Olafson's death. "His cousin, Hilmer Thurman, comes to Cross to take over the family interests. He clearly wants to establish his sway around here, and after Mostek disappears, Thurman makes it known that he wants the Mostek place."

"And this Mostek disappeared after he nearly killed the last sheriff and took some shots at you, I might add," Taters said.

Pilate nodded. "What do you wanna bet that Mostek is dead?"

"Thurman?" Taters said without missing a beat.

"Yeah."

"Okay, but why does he want the store so bad that he'd intimidate the banker with an axe in the back?"

"I don't know. Why wouldn't he just quietly go to Mrs. Mostek and tell her she's to sell the building to him?"

"Maybe she knows that Thurman killed her husband." Taters asked.

"Well, that, and the according to the local scuttlebutt she's been in poor health and doped to the gills most of the time," Pilate said, recalling a rumor he had heard from more than one person around town. "Maybe she washed her hands of the whole thing and told Nemec to handle it…or both." Pilate put the key in the ignition between the front seats and started the car.

"Okay, setting that aside, it looks like the building was first built and owned by an ancestor of this Thurman fella," Taters said. "Do you s'pose that's worth killing over?"

"People have killed for less in this town," Pilate said, backing out of the parking lot, "a lot less."

Chapter Nineteen

“Sheriff, you’d better get over here right now,” Mrs. Drum squawked into his cell phone.

“What’s going on now, Mrs. Drum?”

“What do you think happened? He did it again!” she shouted.

Pilate held the cell out a couple inches from his face. “Did what again?”

“Pooped in my yard!”

“I’m sorry, Mrs. Drum, but what would you like me to do about it?” He felt a distinct stabbing pain in the back of his neck.

“Arrest him!”

“Who?”

“Are you dense, Sheriff? Arrest the person defecating on my property.”

“Who is doing it?”

“What do we pay you for anyway? How the heck do I know?” she said, nearing apoplexy.

Taters chuckled quietly.

Pilate smirked, though the pain in his neck rendered his effort at defiance hollow. “Well, ma’am, unless you see who’s doing it, I really don’t know--”

“Did it on my front porch this time!”

“Oh jeez,” Pilate said. “I’m sorry, Mrs. Drum. I will step up patrols.”

“You’d better, Sheriff.”

“Constable.” Pilate ended the call, the sound of Mrs. Drum slamming her receiver down making him wince. “There’s gotta be a better way to earn this massive salary.”

Taters snickered. “Why you don’t say *adios* to this place and head back down to Key West is beyond me.”

"What would I do there, besides enjoy my life and have fun?"

Taters nodded. "Of course. How silly of me."

* * *

"Commissioner, I need a warrant to search Mostek's store." Pilate heard Ryder inhale deeply through the phone, as if he'd been expecting the request.

"Why?"

"I did some checking, and I think Thurman is definitely behind all this," Pilate said. "I wonder if there's something about that store that's driving this."

"Location, location, location."

"No, not that."

"Like what then?"

"No idea. I just wanna look around."

"Well, go get the keys from the bank. Tell 'em I said so."

"No warrant?"

"No. Just go get the keys, and be discreet," Ryder said. "Let me know what you find," he said, his voice flat.

"Okay. Will do," Pilate tucked the phone in his pocket.

"What?" Taters said.

"I don't know. He seemed...distracted."

"Well, what do we do? Go to a judge or magistrate or something?"

"No. He said we just go back to the bank and get the keys."

"Oh. Well, that's easy. On TV they have to--"

"This isn't CBS, Taters," Pilate said. "How you doing?"

"Me? Fine."

"No pain, no heart stuff?"

Taters shook his head. "Nope, no problem. Let's go, John."

Pilate nosed the Saab in the direction of the bank. "Tonight's martini is gonna be most welcome."

"The backyard bar awaits." Taters smiled. "Ya know, I have to admit that one good thing about this place being as boring as it is...well, it's done wonders for my stress level."

"Yeah, that's one benefit of the smallest town in the world. I--"

Pilate was interrupted by the police radio in his car: "Code One! Code One! Ten-forty-three, Walker Keillor Elementary School. Code One. Ten-forty-three at Walker Keillor Elementary School. All units respond."

Pilate tensed. "Hold on." He slowed the car, then turned around in the middle of the road. He pointed the car the right way and floored the gas pedal.

Taters grasped the door handle tightly. "What the hell? What's a ten-forty-three?"

"One of the codes I had to learn the hard way. Somebody's shooting a gun at Kara's school."

* * *

Pilate gritted his teeth and turned on his emergency light. "Taters, pick up the radio and tell them I'm in transit."

Taters clicked the button a couple times and said, "This is, uh... Constable Pilate. We have received your message and are in hot pursuit to the scene."

"Transit, not pursuit, Rosco P. Coltrane," Pilate whispered. "ETA three minutes."

"Uh...we are in transit to the scene. ETA three minutes," Taters repeated.

"Roger, Constable. Be advised, reserve sheriff deputy at least twelve minutes from scene. State Patrol twenty minutes out. Be advised, responsible is a white male, about thirty-five years old, dark hair, green pants, green jacket, blue tennis shoes."

"Roger," Taters said. "John, what do we do? Wait for the deputy?"

"Hell no. No way. My little girl's in there, damn it."

Subsequent communications reported that the shooter had hit at least two people and was holding a classroom hostage. Fortunately, most of the teachers and students had evacuated safely.

"Taters, get the gun outta the glovebox," Pilate said. "When we crest this next hill, we'll be about 500 feet from the school. I'm gonna stop the car and get out and go around the back of the building. You take the car to the front and help evacuate people. When the deputies arrive, tell them I'm going in, and for God's sake, tell 'em what I'm wearing so they don't shoot me." A trickle of sweat beaded down Pilate's side.

"John, maybe we should wait," Taters said, checking the .38 Smith chamber.

"Can't. This guy's already shot two people, and there's no SWAT team. Those two deputies are good guys, but they're only slightly more qualified than me. Okay, maybe a lot more, but anyway, we don't have time to wait for the State Patrol. Besides, I'm just gonna climb a tree or something out back, and I'll text what I can see from there. I'll set my cell on vibrate, in case they wanna give me instructions. You with me?"

"You never have to ask me that," Taters said. "I just wish I had my .45."

"Me too. There's a shotgun in the trunk, along with a box of shells. Get it. Okay, here we go."

Pilate crested the hill. The school was an anthill of chaos, with teachers, children, and parents running in all directions. Pilate put the car in park, took the gun from Taters, and ran into the woods adjacent to the school.

"Godspeed!" Taters said, running around the back of the car and slipping in to the driver's seat. He felt his chest tightening. "Just cut that out," he said aloud.

Pilate clipped the holster on his belt as he ran through the woods behind the school. He could hear the shouts of kids and teachers as they hustled away from the scene.

"John, we should wait for the professionals," Simon said. *"This is not part of your job description. It's beyond your training...and your competence."*

"Kara, what's my job?" Pilate tried to clear his mind. Kara was likely out front of the school already, out of harm's way. He just had to position himself to give intel to the deputies.

Pilate crawled through the brush beside the school playground, trying to get eyes on the classroom where the gunman was holed up. He couldn't see anything and would have to get closer.

He crawled behind an oak tree and pulled himself to his feet. He spied another large oak not twenty feet from the cafeteria door that opened out to the playground. Scanning the windows again, he still saw no signs of commotion. He could only assume that the shooter was probably in a classroom on the far side of the school.

Pilate broke into a run, covering the distance between the oaks in only a few seconds. Then he ran and flattened himself against the wall beside the cafeteria door. His hands quivered as he fumbled the .38 out of the holster. He gave it a quick look to make sure it was operational, then put his left hand on the cafeteria door.

Pilate gently pulled the door open an inch and peered inside. Dozens of food trays had been hastily abandoned on cafeteria tables, and chairs and food were haphazardly scattered about the gaudy linoleum.

Good. They got out.

Pilate opened the door wider; it groaned on rusty hinges. Pilate froze in place for a moment, then opened it wider, willing the hinges to silence. He slipped in and headed quickly toward the interior door that led to the main hallway. Pilate stepped on the remnants of a peanut butter and jelly sandwich and nearly fell on his ass, but he righted himself and pressed his sweaty torso against the wall beside the door.

"Wait. Doesn't that Robbins kid have a peanut allergy?" Simon said.

Pilate ignored Simon and listened outside of his head. He heard nothing but eerie silence.

"Maybe he surrendered?" Simon volunteered.

"Shut up! Let me think!" A man's voice echoed through the hallway. "Just shut the fuck up and let me think! No more jabbering!"

"Never mind."

Pilate surmised that the gunman was in Corridor B, the same hallway that led to Kara's classroom. He darted out of the cafeteria, into the main hallway, and headed for the corner that turned into Corridor B. The shattered glass of a trophy case crunched under his feet. He winced and stood still. Catty-corner across the hallway were the main doors to the school and the principal's office.

A man's body lay motionless on the floor, his face turned to Pilate, eyes open, glassy and lifeless--he looked surprised. A dark red wound marred his chest.

Pilate next heard the collective murmur of children crying. He felt a vibration in his pocket, a text message from Taters, and he quickly read it: *"Deputies still on the way. Teachers said guy in Army jacket busted in, claiming delivery driver was going to hurt kids. Shot delivery guy and teacher who got in way. Has Glock. Delivery guy may be dead. Teacher bleeding."*

Pilate texted back: *"Dead man in main hallway. I'm 10 feet frm rm. Not sure where kids. Will wait for deps. Which teacher?"*

No sooner had Pilate pushed send than he heard a gunshot and the terrified screams of children.

"Fuck this," he said, bolting down the corridor. A haze of gunsmoke filtered from a classroom; it was Abbey's class.

Pilate saw a smear of blood just outside the door, as if someone had been shot in the hallway and dragged inside. He slowed and looked for something he could throw. He scooped up a *Dora the Explorer* backpack from the floor and inched to the door of the room. He heard children crying and the familiar voice of Abbey Prince.

"Please, mister, you have to let the kids go," she pleaded, her voice quavering.

"I-I was just doing my job," the man said, stammering. "The kids were not safe."

Pilate crouched low, peeking into the room. Packed into a corner were at least ten kids, crying, and a man pacing back and forth past a prone and bleeding Abbey Prince.

The man looked vaguely familiar, but Pilate couldn't see his face. The collar on his Army jacket was turned up, obscuring his profile. Abbey was holding her right side, and the bright red blood oozing between her fingers wasn't a good sign.

Pilate knew he was nowhere near a good enough shot to take the guy out without risking hitting the kids or Abbey, but he also knew he had to do something.

His cell vibrated again: *"Dep outside in tree sez he has a shot at guy. can you distract?"*

"Yes," Pilate texted.

"Dep sez if u distract, he will take shot."

"OK. What do I do?"

"Count to 30 and get guy away from kids. Godspeed."

Pilate inhaled a shallow breath and replied, "Yes," then began his countdown.

Shit! Do I say "Mississippi" between each number?

"It doesn't matter now, John. Just count to thirty," Simon said.

Pilate counted, grasping the backpack and the .38. He slid up to his full height.

Twenty-one, twenty-two…

He hadn't seen Kara in there, but it was hard to make out any faces.

Twenty-four, twenty-five...

God help me.

Twenty-nine…

Pilate burst into the room and threw the backpack at the gunman. It hit him on the back, startling him, and he turned to face Pilate.

"Rich?" Pilate sputtered at the neighborhood watch captain.

Rich blinked and raised the Glock in Pilate's direction.

"No, Gary!" Pilate yelled.

"Where's that fucking deputy?" Simon shouted in Pilate's brain.

On cue, the deputy fired, shattering the window.

Gary Rich grunted as the bullet grazed his shoulder. He fell back, still grasping the Glock, waving it wildly at the terrified students.

Pilate was five feet from Rich. Clutching his revolver, he threw himself at him, slamming him into a bookshelf and knocking the Glock from Rich's hand. Pilate smacked Rich across the face with his pistol, knocking him out.

The kids shrieked in fear and relief as Pilate rolled Rich on his belly and pulled his arms behind his back. Pilate pinned Rich's arms down by planting his knee on them.

He turned and saw Abbey smiling at him, trying to get up. "No! Stay put, Abbey. Just stay there," Pilate said.

In seconds, the room filled with two deputies, followed closely by Burl Crites and another paramedic Pilate didn't recognize, both carrying heavy gear.

The deputy patted Pilate's shoulder. "Good work, Constable. I'll cuff him."

Pilate nodded, holstered his gun, and knelt beside Abbey. He looked at Burl hopefully, and Burl returned the hopeful look.

"Thanks, Sheriff," Abbey said, trying to smile.

"That's Cons--"

He was interrupted by a hug around his neck.

"Daddy!" Kara squealed. "You were right about your job. You kept me safe!"

"Thank God," Pilate said. "Are you okay, baby?"

Kara nodded and wiped tears from her eyes. "I was scared, but I knew you would save us, even without this." She proudly pointed at his badge, still pinned to her shirt.

"What's my job?"

"To keep me safe," she said, smiling. "And everybody else."

Chapter Twenty

"Why didn't you shoot the son-of-a-bitch?" Ryder asked.

"Like I told you before, I don't ever plan to shoot at anybody again," Pilate said, repressing the urge to knock Ryder on his ass. "Besides, the kids were in the line of fire, and I'm not a good shot."

"Sir, Miss Prince is at the hospital. They're prepping her for surgery," a reserve deputy said as he strung crime scene tape around the school steps.

Ryder nodded. "Good shooting," he said to the deputy, who nodded and went back to work.

Pilate glanced at Taters, who was holding Kara just a few feet away, beside the Saab. Pilate felt the adrenaline draining from his body.

"Didn't mean to criticize, John," Ryder said, his voice just above a whisper, clasping Pilate's shoulder a moment.

Pilate nodded, looked around the scene, then glanced back to Ryder. "I know. How the hell did a nut like that get access to a gun?"

"Second Amendment," Ryder said, shrugging.

"Yeah, well, that's just great. A delusional idiot breezes in here with a gun, kills a man, shoots a teacher, and God knows what else he could've done. He had three clips of fifteen on him. But yeah, we have to let that happen 'cause the British may invade us at any moment, right?" Pilate felt his adrenaline boiling over again, his vision red and closing in like a camera aperture.

Ryder looked at him dispassionately.

"Well?"

"Well what?"

"Is that all the fuck you have to say? 'Second Amendment'?"

"For now, yes."

"Ya know, Ryder, you're one cold son-of-a…" Pilate pointed a finger at Ryder.

Trooper Hulsey strode up. His eyes darted from Pilate's red face to his index finger and Ryder's cool, expressionless face. "Excuse me, gentlemen," he said, pointing at Gary Rich, who was handcuffed in the back of Hulsey's patrol car. "We're gonna run the shooter to the hospital. Once the docs have that arm all patched up, we'll take him over to the cookie factory."

"Screw that. He may be mental, but I want him put in stir," Ryder said.

Hulsey rocked back on his heels a moment. "Commissioner, he's a nut-bag. It's best we throw his butt in secure mental lockup, a damn straightjacket and a rubber room."

Ryder shook his head. "No. Put him in the can, and make sure every con in there knows he tried to kill some kids." Ryder's blue eyes took on a steely, blank quality.

Hulsey shrugged. "I'm state police, Commissioner. I take orders from my colonel, and he says the gunman goes to the hospital, then to secure psych for eval." Hulsey didn't wait for a reply; instead, he turned and took two steps away before turning back. "Hell of a brave thing you did in there, John. You never cease to amaze us, buddy."

"Um…thanks?"

"I think he meant it as a compliment, tenderfoot," Ryder drawled.

Hulsey nodded and walked to his cruiser.

Pilate locked eyes with Gary Rich, who bucked up and down, screaming in the back seat. His mouth was moving, but no sound could penetrate the bulletproof glass.

Ryder chuckled. "Damn. Hulsey's too by-the-book for the shit, but I had to try," he said.

"Look, I'm sorry--"

"No you're not, and you don't gotta be." Ryder's eyes changed subtly, becoming a little less steely, flintier.

"John! John! Kara!"

Pilate turned to the edge of a cordon and saw Kate breaking through the police tape. She grabbed Kara from Taters, fell to her knees, and hugged her as if she never wanted to let her go.

"Mommy, you're squishing me," Kara whined.

"I'm sorry, baby. I'm just so glad you're all right," Kate said, and both of them broke down in tears.

"Commissioner, I need to--"

"Go," Ryder said. "We'll talk later."

Pilate knelt beside his family, melting into the embrace. Tears welled in his eyes. It was a bit of a struggle to clear the massive lump that had formed in his throat.

"Mommy, Daddy did it."

"What, honey?" Kate asked, wiping tears from her eyes.

"He kept me safe. It's his job."

Kate looked at Pilate. "He did, didn't he? He's very good at it." She laughed and kissed him.

Pilate smiled, kissed his wife, then looked away, back at the school.

"Stop, John. You know as well as I do that you can't protect them everywhere, Daddy Dearest," Simon scolded.

"Here, Daddy," Kara said, pinning the badge crookedly on his sweaty, bloodstained shirt.

"Oh," he said softly. "Thank you." The weight of the brass badge made his pocket droop.

"John, you okay?" Kate said.

"Yeah, sweetheart. I'm fine. I just need to make sure Abbey's all right."

"Go on over to the hospital with Taters. I'll take Kara home, and we'll all be together tonight."

Pilate felt like he was starring in a movie, some sort of Monday afternoon matinee about his own life, as if he had lines to say but was unsure of the inflection. What he did know was that all the anger he had felt toward Ryder was gone. "Okay, babe," he said, hugging his girls again. "Kate, Kara, I love you."

Kate's tears flowed again. "Thank you so much for saving our baby. I-I love you," she said with a sniffle.

Pilate felt an aw-shucks-'twern't-nothin'-ma'am comment coming on, but he stifled it. He merely nodded, winked at his little girl, and walked over to Taters, who was leaning on the Saab, chatting with Ryder.

Ryder wordlessly tipped his hat to them both as Pilate approached and walked away, loping along in ostrich boots.

"Interesting guy," Taters said, watching Ryder go.

"To say the least," Pilate said. "Thanks, pal."

"What for?"

"You and I worked together on this, and you know it."

Taters waved Pilate off. "Texting? Please. I think you got the raw end of the deal this time."

"Bullshit. I heard. You took charge of the scene until the deputies arrived. Ryder said you ordered all the kids and teachers to head for the barn in that cornfield across the road. You got them to safety, and then you helped orchestrate the raid on that psycho."

Taters looked down at his feet. "Aw shucks. Just helpin' out, Boss."

"Hey…you okay?" Pilate said.

Taters sighed and sounded perturbed as he answered, "If you're askin' if all this excitement gave me a heart attack, no. I'm right as rain."

"Good, we're heading to the hospital now to check on Abbey, so if you need a shock or a defibrillation or whatever, I can make that happen. I know people."

"Pssh. Just get in your damn girlie car, Mr. Small-town Hero," Taters said, opening the passenger door. "Shock me my ass."

* * *

"She'll have a nasty scar on her side, but the bullet missed the vitals," Head Nurse Juilie Hulsey said in the waiting area. "Doc Hutton says that aside from being shot, she's a lucky young lady."

"That's great news," Pilate said. "When can I see her?"

"She's still out of it, and it's family only for a while anyway, so…"

"I guess that leaves me out," a voice from behind Pilate said, breaking.

Pilate turned to face a shaken Riley Pierson, doing his best to hold himself together. "Riley, she's okay," Pilate said.

"Oh my God, Mr. Pilate, Abbey nearly died, and I was so mean to her." His eyes were red and watery. "I really hurt her, and now she's--"

"Gonna be fine, Nebraska," Pilate said. He grasped Riley's shoulders. "Look at me, pal."

Riley sniffled and quickly wiped his eyes with a fist, looking at Pilate.

"You didn't do this to her, and what she needs now is our strength, so she can get well. Understand?"

Riley nodded sadly, looking down at the tile floor.

"Why don't you come back tomorrow?"

"No. I'm staying here until she wakes up."

Pilate nodded. "Good man. Juilie, can Riley wait?"

"Of course," she said. "If Abbey's folks decide it's okay, and if she wants to see you, you can. It will be a few hours, though, maybe not even till tomorrow."

"I don't care. I'm not leaving. I want her to know I'm here for her."

Pilate clapped Riley on the back.

Riley offered a sheepish smile, wandered over to an orange pleather chair, and fell heavily into it like a sack of potatoes.

"What about Gary Rich?"

Juilie made a face. "That creep? He got seven stitches. He also has a bump on his head and a shiner that would put Lee Harvey Oswald to shame. Nice work. Mike took him over to the mental unit at county. He's not all there. And speaking of nuts, what about you?"

"Me? Oh, just a bruise here and there."

"Hmm. Maybe you oughtta leave your diagnosis up to the professionals. Come on in the exam room and take your shirt off, and I'll look you over."

Pilate shook his head. "Not necessary. Thanks though. I'm sure there's a mountain of paperwork to do on this, so I'd better get to it. I'll check on Abbey tomorrow."

"No problem, Constable," Juilie said, winking and heading back to her station.

"Now I bet she's got some good…bedside manner," Taters said, shaking his head. "You shoulda let her examine you."

Pilate chuckled, clapped his friend on the shoulder, and headed for the door. "C'mon, Romeo," he said.

* * *

"Oh my God, I can't believe you're on the news again," Monique said, her studied New York City cool shaken by the news of the school shooting. "You saved some kids!"

Pilate sighed a bit, trying to think of something clever to say, but nothing came to mind. He shifted the phone from one ear to the other.

"John? Hey, old man, you there?"

"Yeah," Pilate said, looking at his boots on the linoleum of his kitchen floor. An untouched drink sat on the counter.

"You okay?" Monique asked in an oddly serious tone.

"Yeah, Monique. Just a tough day," Pilate said. He envied Taters, who was outside, in the fresh air, leaning against the Frontdoor Backyard Bar, Modelo in hand. "What's up?"

"Oh. Well, I'm just calling to tell you that you might finally be achieving sexy with all this heroism. You have a real Harrison Ford thing going, ya know? Old but kinda hot? Do you have a Fedora and a whip? Wait. If you've got a whip, I don't wanna hear about it."

Pilate laughed, a genuine chuckle. "Yeah, me and Indiana Solo, we're like peas in a sexy AARP pod."

"You act more like Rick Deckard," Simon chimed in.

"Well, if we can table the geriatric sexiness discussion for a minute," she said, chuckling herself, "I have some news."

"Frechette, hopefully. Did they catch him? Do you have my money for me?"

"No, not yet. Sorry. He's still on the lam, leaving a trail of empty sidecars in his wake, but I'm sure they'll catch up to him eventually."

"So what's the news?"

"You. You're national news again, and that made the phone ring. I put the word out about your new book, but I didn't hear a peep till you went all Rambo this afternoon. Now I have three fishing calls and one full-fledged offer."

Pilate eyed the drink. "My, my, how...predictable of them."

"Don't look a gift horse in the ass, John," she said. "The advance offer is $50,000."

"That's pretty good," Pilate said, whistling.

"Yeah, but it's not good enough. Let me keep at it. By the way, Angee called and griped at me for stealing you away from her as a client."

"Stealing me away? But she ditched me."

"I know, right? She cray-cray."

"Yeah, she's always been a little...self-absorbed."

"Okay. Well, now that the excitement is over out there, you'd better get cracking on that sequel."

"Uh..." Pilate rubbed the back of his neck, squeezing it, trying to force it to pop or move a little. He was quickly developing a beauty of a headache. "About that..."

Monique inhaled deeply, let it out in short bursts, and cleared her throat. "You haven't written anything, have you?"

"Not exactly."

"What?"

"I'm working on it, just not much yet and not what you asked for."

"Oh. Well, in that case..." she said.

"It's not a nonfiction follow up. It's a...well, it's kind of more like a novel."

"A novel?"

"Mm-hmm."

"About?"

"Well, me, I guess, the whole magilla, just fictionalized. Don't be mad, Monique."

"I'm not about to get shitty with a legit hero, John."

"Stop."

"In fact..." She paused, smacked her lips, and continued. "If I'm hearing you correctly, you will actually be able to tell your story in a sexier way by fictionalizing some of it. I mean, disguising it as fiction, you could actually do some things that are more...interesting."

"Yeah, I mean really, a decades-old murder mystery, attempts on my family's life, an attack by pirates on the open water, a psychopath chasing me across the country, a school shooting? Yeah, I can see where a novel would be more interesting."

"Hmm," she purred, not rising to the bait. "I like it. Could even be a series. Lemme see what I can do. I'll work the hero angle in and see if we can sell it."

"Thanks, little girl," Pilate said.

"Ick. You went there, you dirty old man."

"What did Indy say? 'It's not the years, honey. It's the mileage.'"

"Gross."

"You started it. Now, if you'll excuse me, I have a cocktail to drink, and you need to go have private thoughts about Harrison Ford."

"Ass," she said, then hung up.

Pilate scooped up the martini and looked into the living room. Kate was asleep on the sofa, the kids asleep upstairs, so he crept quietly outside.

"Cheers, buddy," he said to Taters.

"What kept you?"

"The promise of money and talk about sex…and bullwhips."

"Fair enough."

Chapter Twenty-One

The smell of dust, rotten food, and blood still permeated the air in Mostek's General Store, where former Sheriff Welliver nearly lost his life in a shootout with the now missing, presumed-dead, Perry Mostek.

"Mmm. Fragrant," Taters said, walking into a sunbeam that broke through a tear in the butcher paper covering the closed store's glass edifice.

"The Mostek family cleaned it up a few days after the state police released the scene back to them, but by the looks of things, they only managed to remove most of the stock and do a quick mop of the floor." Pilate pointed to the area where Welliver nearly bled out.

"Yeah, that stain's gonna hang around a while longer, unless somebody gets some elbow grease and bleach on it," Taters said.

"Uh-huh." Pilate surveyed the empty shelves, which made ghostly shadows under the flickering fluorescent lights. He signaled Taters to follow him.

"That the office?"

"Yup, right up these stairs."

They looked around the office, which was still furnished with a small desk and some empty filing cabinets. On the wall, hanging crookedly, was a map of Cross Township. The office was almost round, as it occupied the turret-shaped second floor of the building.

"Nothing," Taters said. "No safe, no secret panels."

"Well, that's no surprise. Let's go back downstairs."

"What are we looking for?" Taters asked, opening the lid and peering into the beer and soda fridge beside the cash register. A sign advertising a sale on Bud was taped to the side.

"I don't know." Pilate stamped his foot on the creaky wooden floor. "I was kind of hoping to find a trapdoor or something. I guess that was silly."

Taters closed the fridge. "Maybe you're just not looking in the right place."

"Well, I've looked at every square inch of the bare floor, and the shelves are bolted down, so--"

"How about a beer?"

"Taters, it's only ten a.m. Beer isn't the answer to everything," Pilate said, shaking his head.

"You sure 'bout that?" Taters gestured at the beer fridge, then squatted beside it.

"What?" Pilate walked over, looking at a groove on the floor that Taters touched with a fingertip.

"Looks like this fridge has been moved a few times, and I don't think Modelo or Bud or Boulevard Wheat had anything to do with it."

The fridge was heavy and unwieldy, but Taters and Pilate moved it with minimum effort. Pilate did his best to do most of the pushing to slide it over, sparing Taters any unnecessary exertion.

"You okay?"

"Ask me that one more time, and I'll knock you on your ass, John."

Pilate smiled. "Okay, okay."

Pilate went to his car and retrieved two flashlights, keeping an eye out to make sure no one was watching. Satisfied that there were no prying eyes, he hurried back inside the store and locked the store door behind him, eager to check out what was beneath the fridge-concealed trapdoor. "Here," he said, handing one of the flashlights to Taters.

"Got your gun?"

"Why would I need a gun in a general store basement?" Pilate said, shining his light into the hole and revealing an ancient wooden ladder. "God. I'm starting to feel like Indiana Jones."

"Huh?"

"Nothing."

"I'll go first."

"Sorry, pal. It's my job. I'll take point," Pilate said, easing down through the trapdoor, testing the rungs of the ladder. "Feels okay, but doesn't look like anybody's been in here for a while." He continued to descend, shining the light at the bottom. "Looks like it's only about ten feet down. C'mon."

Pilate climbed the rest of the way down, his senses overcome by a moldy, cold, dusty smell. He held the ladder as Taters climbed down.

"John, the ladder's bolted to the wall. Let go and move over." Taters hopped down from the last two rungs, shining his flashlight around the room.

It looked like a partially finished basement, complete with a partially exposed wood subfloor, cobwebs, and dirt. The walls had old wood paneling in places, but they were mostly comprised of exposed rock.

"Charming," Pilate said, "but let's see what we can see down here." Pilate wandered around the room for a few seconds, shining his beam on the walls. He caught what felt like a cool breeze across his cheek. "You feel that?"

Taters mumbled assent.

"Start feeling around. That breeze didn't come from the trapdoor."

Pilate and Taters tapped the walls, which appeared to be gray and solid amidst the monochrome gloom.

"That's weird. I don't think there's a vent or--" Suddenly, Taters fell forward, as if he was intentionally trying to collide with the wall. "Ouch!"

"Taters! Hey, you okay?" Pilate asked, hurrying over to his friend, who was on the floor, covered in a dirty curtain of muslin.

"Yeah, but look what I found, Scooby. A secret passageway."

Pilate felt the breeze on his face again. He helped Taters to his feet, and both men shined their lights into the passageway. Hewn from the rock, it was three feet wide and varied in height but seemed to be about five feet tall in most places.

Stooping, Pilate walked forward a few feet, shining his light on an old sconce. "Wow. This looks pretty old."

"Yeah, a real temple of doom, huh, Constable Indy?" Taters's light exposed another sconce a few feet away on the other side of the passage. "There's a candle stub in this one. This is some real *Great Escape* stuff, man, except way roomier."

"Looks like it goes on for quite a ways," Pilate said. "You up for it?"

Taters shrugged. "Sure, but I wish you'd brought your gun."

After working their way through at least 200 yards of cramped, cobwebbed passage, the pair arrived at the terminus.

"Well, shit."

"Don't go no farther?" Taters asked.

"Nope. Just sorta…quits," Pilate said. "At least here, we can stand without stooping."

"This don't make sense."

"I know. Maybe they gave up. I mean, it's unfinished. Or maybe it caved in."

"You're forgetting something, Constable," Taters said, pointing around in the air.

Pilate snapped his fingers. "The breeze! Of course. There has to be some way outta of here."

"Said the joker to the--"

"Look!" Pilate pointed his light up, revealing a wooden door in the ceiling, about seven feet off the ground. He saw small cracks in and around the door; they apparently allowed for airflow when both ends of the passage were clear.

"The last tourists to these caverns musta pulled the ladder up with them," Taters said.

"Crap," Pilate said, shining his light at the floor. "I didn't think to keep an eye out for footprints. Do you see any?"

"Oops, Columbo. Just ours, I think."

"Well, we'll have to look more carefully later. For now, we need to see what's on the other side of that door."

"I'm lighter than you. Gimme a boost," Taters said. "Doc told me not to do any heavy lifting."

"No, that won't do. Let me get on all fours, and you try to reach from my back. But if a rat saunters by, you may get a headache from me launching you into the ceiling. I hate rats."

"Got it," Taters said, putting the flashlight in his back pocket and stepping onto Pilate's back.

"Oomph," Pilate groaned. "How in the hell does Jordan tolerate you on top of her?"

"I'll try to forget you said that," Taters said, adding a couple grunts as he balanced on Pilate's back and reached for the door. His fingertips brushed the wooden slats.

"Get it?"

"Not quite," Taters said, reaching again, stretching his arm. "Dang."

"A little more alacrity, if you please, Taters," Pilate said, gasping.

Taters pulled the small Maglite from his back pocket and used it to extend his reach. It made a decidedly solid *thump* on the wood. "Hit it, but it ain't moving any. There might be something on it, a case of beer or something."

"Okay. Get down then," Pilate said with another grunt.

"You sure?"

"Get off me, Taters."

"That's what she said." Taters snickered, climbed off Pilate's back, and helped him to his feet.

Pilate brushed the dirt from his knees and palms. "Crap. Well, we'll have to go get a ladder or something."

"And do what? I mean, we have no idea where this goes. How are we gonna explain ourselves if we open it up and climb into some nice lady's boudoir or something? Catch her *in flagrante delicto*?"

"God, Taters, you really need to get laid," Pilate said, "but you're right. Besides, we can easily figure this out by counting the paces and checking it out topside."

"I hope it opens up to someplace that serves them conch fritters."

"Fat chance. If my calculations are correct, I think we'll actually be somewhere that serves something…a wee bit stronger."

* * *

Cusack slid a double-shot of Jameson's across the bar to Pilate and Taters. "For our hero," he said, his eyes twinkling.

Pilate had just started to introduce Taters to Cusack when he held up a hand, poured the drinks, and presented them to the pair.

"Cusack, this isn't necessary," Pilate protested, with little enthusiasm.

Taters picked up his tumbler of whiskey and inhaled the aroma. "Much obliged."

Cusack poured himself a shot and held up his glass. "To John and Taters, who saved the day."

Pilate flushed, embarrassed, but clinked glasses and drank half the contents. "Thanks. We were just--"

"Doing our jobs," Taters finished, a poor Clint Eastwood impression.

Cusack glanced around the bustling bar. "Well, in any case, glad you stitched up that bastard. Well done."

Pilate nodded.

"So what brings you over here this time of day?" Cusack said. "Trying to beat the lunch rush or all those OakFest folks?"

"Not exactly," Pilate said, putting his glass down. "We were wondering if we could have a look at your basement."

Chapter Twenty-Two

"I dunno what you tink you'll find down here," Cusack said, grunting as he moved aside boxes. "I've never noticed any door in the floor or nothin'."

Pilate helped move some of the boxes across the wooden floor, looking for any unexpected entryways to another chamber. "Hmm. Maybe it's not even a door at all. Coulda been floor we saw."

Taters nodded.

"You found a passageway leading from the store to here?" Cusack asked, scratching his head. "Odd."

Pilate stopped staring at the floorboards. "Odder still, when you think of the coincidence."

"Coincidence?"

"Well, yeah. The tunnel or passage or whatever you call it leads from this bed-and-breakfast you currently own, to the general store you're trying to buy."

"'Tis odd, John, no doubt about it."

Pilate folded his arms. "Cusack, be honest with me. Did you know about this or not?"

"No," he said emphatically, his eyes going from Pilate to Taters and back again. "Well…not exactly."

"What does that mean?"

"John, I have the situation well in hand, as you say here in the U.S. of A.," Cusack assured him, a tinge of irritation evident in his usually jovial demeanor. His knotty hands rested at his sides, his fingernails dirty.

"Cusack, I'm the law in this town." Instantly, Pilate felt idiotic just saying it, and he knew Simon was no doubt in hysterics somewhere in his cerebral cortex, but he continued, "I'm investigating an attempted murder of the man who controls the sale of that store and, incidentally, holds the note on your place."

Cusack threw his hands up in the stagnant air. "All right Copper, you got me," he said, then plopped himself down on a box, releasing a frustrated sigh.

Pilate and Taters leaned against the basement wall, waiting for Cusack to spill the beans.

"I've only been down there once, and I couldn't believe it when I found out it goes from here to the store. I mean, it has to be an old bootlegger's passage, if ya get my meanin'."

"Yeah. So?"

"So…it would be a helluva ting, ya know, for the punters."

"What?" Taters said.

"You know, a proper tourist attraction. 'Visit the secret bootlegger's tunnel beneath Cross Township,' that sorta ting," Cusack smiled. "Like that town in Kansas. Atchison, I believe? The most haunted town in the state? You know how much money a gimmick like that brings in?"

"So you wanna buy the store why?" Pilate said, not really getting the concept.

"That's what's really grand. I want to make it a proper restaurant and bar, not like the wee bar I have upstairs. A real swanky place, maybe with a speakeasy in the basement. There are loads of possibilities, and the tunnel will draw people in."

"Loads of money-makin' potential, for sure," Taters acknowledged.

"Yeah," Pilate said, deflated.

Cusack looked up at the men standing over him. "Well, cheer up, boys. It's not the end of the world."

"No, no, sorry, Cusack," Pilate said. "It just seems a little… I don't know. Like a bit of an anticlimax. But wait. What about groceries for the people in Cross? Are you saying if you get this, you aren't gonna sell milk, eggs, bread, and diapers?"

"Hell no. That's too much work for me. There's plenty of room 'round here for somebody else to build a new store." He beamed. "I mean, really, how boring would that be?"

"Maybe you've got a point, buddy," Taters drawled. "I mean, the last grocer apparently liked to moonlight as an assassin."

Pilate and Taters asked Cusack a few more questions, including some about his relationship with Hilmer Thurman, whom Cusack swore he'd never met. Pilate thanked Cusack for his time and walked back to the Saab with Taters.

* * *

"So, let's see. We've got an Irish dude who wants to buy the town general store, which includes a secret underground passage," Taters said on the short walk from the Cross and Cork to the constable's office. "From a Polish family who bought the property from a Swedish guy who's an ancestor of the town crime boss."

"Sounds about right, Taters," Pilate said with a nod.

"And the banker behind the whole thing caught an axe blade in the back why?" Taters asked Pilate from across the Saab roof.

"Good question," Pilate opened the door and climbed into the driver's seat.

"Unless this Thurman guy did it because he wanted to kill Nemec to keep him from screwing up the sale of the store," Taters mused.

"Maybe he wasn't trying to kill him. Maybe he really was trying to send a message."

"To who?"

"Everyone involved."

"But Cusack denies even knowing Thurman."

"I know, but I think he was lying through his teeth."

* * *

Leaning back in his chair and staring up at the ceiling of the constable's office, Taters asked, "Are those pencils up there?"

"Yeah."

"What the hell, John?"

Pilate shrugged and harrumphed. "I get bored."

"Well, you ain't got no time to throw pencils now," Taters said. "You've got a mystery to solve, Copper."

"Something's not adding up here. I guess I'm gonna have to have a word with Hilmer Thurman."

"Cool," Taters said. "I wanna meet that cat."

"Sorry, but I think you'll need to keep your distance on this one, pal," Pilate said.

"What? Why? You deputized me, remember?"

"Let's go over to the college cafeteria, and I'll think about it."

"Nothin' to tink about," Taters said, aping Cusack's accent. "I'm going."

* * *

Kate joined them for lunch.

"How's our girl?"

Kate ran a hand through her dirty-blonde hair. "She's so tough. Since school's out for a few more days while they clean up the mess that nut made, I asked her if she wants to stay home with me. She prefers to help out at daycare here."

"I think she's feeling protective of Peter," Pilate said. "She wants to make sure her baby brother's okay."

"I think the phrase is 'keep him safe.'" She smiled. "I can't tell you both how glad I am you were there. Jesus, it coulda been so much worse."

Taters winked.

"I wish I had been more proactive about that guy," Pilate said. "I mean, I knew he was a whack-job, but I had no idea how dangerous he was."

"Hell, can we really tell these days?" Taters said. "I mean, there's a fine line between crazy and eccentric."

Pilate nodded. "Yeah, like Harley Cordwainer. He's eccentric. No, wait. He's both."

"It doesn't help that it's practically easier to get a handgun than it is to get a driver's license," Kate said, her jaw set. "Insanity. Sometimes I think we live in a damned armed madhouse instead of a civilized country."

"Easy now, Kate," Taters said. "Most gun owners are good folks, and--"

"Okay, let's not go there," Pilate said. "Not now, okay?"

"'Course, John. Sorry, Kate."

She nodded. "Been a tough--"

"Week?" Taters offered.

"Week? Yeah. Try year," Kate said. "Nearly killed a couple times over. It isn't easy when your mortality is constantly thrown in your face."

Pilate could hardly argue with her, and her flash of temper was the sign of someone who had been living with the pall of trauma, death, anxiety and the threat of violence over her life.

"Too true, my dear," Taters said, putting a hand over his heart without realizing it. "Too true."

"I'm sorry, Taters," Kate said. "I know you've ducked a few bullets yourself."

"Not another word about it, sweetheart," Taters said.

Pilate pushed his plate away.

"Not hungry?" Taters asked rhetorically.

Pilate shook his head.

Kate sipped her iced tea for a moment, absently eyeing the students coming and going. "Halloween dance next week," she said.

"OakFest this week," Pilate said. "Which reminds me, I need to see a man about an axe."

* * *

"Just wait in the car," Pilate said, his hands on the steering wheel, parked in front of the Brown Betty.

"Jeez. Can you at least crack the window so I don't get too hot?" Taters said. "C'mon, John. I won't say a word. Just let me go in for backup."

"It's not dangerous, Taters," Pilate said, opening the car door.

"Then why are you wearing your gun?"

Chapter Twenty-Three

Thurman sat at the bar instead of the usual perch in his office. Scanning a copy of *The Cross Courier*, he peered over his reading glasses into the mirror, catching Pilate and Taters as they made an entrance. Also unusual was the silent jukebox and the absence of the leathery Nelda. In fact, save the three men, the Brown Betty Roadhouse was empty.

"Hello, Constable," Thurman said, not moving his head or his hands. The newspaper remained up, his eyes glued to the page.

"Mr. Thurman," Pilate said, stopping at the door and surveying the rest of the room.

"Nice badge," Thurman said, his head still frozen as if held in an invisible vice. "Who's your friend?"

"Name's Malley," Taters said.

"Well, Constable, Mr. Malley, what can I do for you?" His eyes danced over the headlines.

"Got any Modelo?" Taters asked, earning an elbow from Pilate.

"We don't serve that Mexican swill," Thurman said, smiling.

Taters took umbrage but stayed quiet.

"Got time for a little chat?" Pilate asked, folding his arms, which had the effect of pushing his badge out over his forearm. It gleamed in the soft glow of the silent jukebox and beer-pushing neon lining the walls.

The newspaper fell to the bar, and Thurman was on his feet, removing his reading glasses and walking behind the bar in a motion so fluid that Pilate nearly reached for his sidearm. "Coffee?" he offered, filling a red University of Nebraska Huskers mug for himself.

"No thanks."

Taters also demurred.

"Well, c'mon over, and let's have this little chat of yours," Thurman said, sipping from the Huskers mug.

Pilate walked to the bar and eased himself onto the stool that had been vacated by Thurman. *The Cross Courier* was open to the story about Gary Rich's assault on the school. Pilate closed the paper and pushed it aside.

"Nice work, there, Constable," Thurman said. "You just keep surprising us with your heroics. Maybe I oughtta ask for your autograph on that there paper."

Taters sat beside Pilate, facing the empty room rather than Thurman. "Don't surprise me one bit," he said. "John's a decent guy who does the right thing."

"Don't we all?" Thurman said, smiling into his mug.

"No, not all of us, sir," Taters sniffed. "If we all did, John wouldn't have to be a hero, now would he?"

"Okay, Mr. Thurman, look. I need to talk to you about Parker Nemec."

"How's the ol' boy doing?" Thurman placed the mug on the bar and leaned on its scarred wooden surface with both hands.

"He's alive," Pilate said. "The question is, why did somebody mistake him for a piece of firewood?"

Thurman shrugged. "Dunno. Maybe because he's about as interesting as a stick of mesquite."

"Mesquite?" Pilate said. "That reminds me. I seem to recall that your friend Otis, over at the Tin Roof, is known for being handy with chopping wood."

"Not my circus. Not my monkies," Thurman corrected, pinching the end of his nose for a second, and then putting his hand back on the bar. "I play poker with him on occasion, but that's about it."

"Hmm," Pilate said. "Well, we can't seem to find him."

"So look harder."

"I hear Cusack, the Irishman, is bidding on the Mostek store."

Thurman remained impassive, regarding Pilate without saying word.

"And I hear you are too."

Thurman grunted, his face still blank.

"Big talker, aren't ya?" Taters said.

"I suppose I am when there's somebody worth talking to," Thurman said. "Not some wannabe hero and his trailer-trash pal from Key West."

Taters rose to his feet. "Sir, with all due disrespect, fuck you."

Pilate put his hand on his short-tempered, bad-tickered friend's arm. "Taters, go wait outside, pal."

Taters jerked away, keeping his eyes on Thurman's. "No, asshole. If you wanna dance, I'm your huckleberry."

"Taters…" Pilate said, his voice deadly still.

Taters backed off.

"See ya," Thurman said. "I'll call you if I get any of that wetback juice in stock."

Taters stormed out, leaving the front door ajar.

"See what you did, Thurman? You went and insulted a nice guy," Pilate said. "That's not like you, not very…gentlemanly at all."

Thurman breathed in and out deeply. He took another sip of coffee, looked around the bar, then stared at Pilate. His eyes betrayed a heaviness Pilate hadn't observed previously. "John, I thought we had an understanding," Thurman said, his voice quiet and measured.

"Which was?"

"You mind you're business, for starters. Also, that we're even."

"Even? So it *was* you?"

"Yeah, even," Thurman said. "Don't be coy. We're both men of the world, but there is one difference between me and you."

"More than one, but what are you saying?"

"I'm here to stay, and you ain't."

"What's that supposed to mean? Another poorly disguised threat, Thurman?"

Thurman nodded at Pilate's chest. "Don't let that badge give you any ideas. You're still the blundering, ridiculous ass today that you were the day you arrived in Cross."

Pilate felt butterflies dancing the lambada in his stomach. "You wound me."

"Let me finish." Thurman held up an index finger before him, looking all the world like a street hypnotist plying his trade. "I give you a lotta latitude 'round here for a lotta reasons. One is, despite my critical words, I've got a grudging respect for your survival instincts."

Pilate nodded.

"But that latitude ends where my interests begin. I'm sure a man like you can appreciate a little…self-preservation." Thurman folded his arms across his chest and cocked his head. "See, I have some plans for this town, and they include purchasing the old Mostek store."

"So that's why you killed Perry Mostek? To get your hands on his store?"

"Stop it, John. Provocation of that nature is unnecessary." He flashed his synthetic, pearly smile a moment. "That building has sentimental value to my family, and I intend to get it back. That Mick wants to build a fucking bar there, and that isn't gonna happen. There's already enough drinkin' going on in this town."

"Yeah, well, his little bar at the B&B is always full," Pilate said, looking mockingly around at all the empty chairs. He also watched for signs of life from the door to Thurman's office, but he saw no movement. "Anyway, that house is that important to you? You're willing to try to murder a banker and God knows what else?"

"No. Even if it were that valuable to me," Thurman said, shifting his weight from foot to foot, "what's it to you?"

Pilate tapped his badge.

Thurman rolled his eyes.

"What do you really want, Thurman? Are you after that house or what's under it?"

Thurman's eyebrows rose in surprise. "My, my, my." He laughed. "You surprise me yet again. Yes, I want what's under it too."

"What for?"

"I'm a doomsday prepper. That's where I plan to go when the zombie apocalypse dawns."

Pilate nodded slowly. "Uh-huh."

"Constable, suffice it to say I want it. Why is none of your fucking business. Now, I suggest you get back in your lovely little Swedish car--which I think is swell, by the way--and go back to town and quit sniffing around out here. I hear you write books. Why not go someplace warm, like Florida. Take your wife and kids and your strange pal out there, pack a typewriter, and write to your little heart's content on some sunny beach."

"Great idea," Simon said.

"Love to," Pilate said, "but I have a job to do."

Thurman shook his head. "Tedious. This won't end well if you keep pushing, ya know."

"Again with the threats, Thurman?" Pilate said, pushing back from the bar and standing, his guts roiling like the Gulf waves that toss Taters's boat around.

Thurman shook his head. "Nope. I don't have to threaten you."

"I'd say you just did," Pilate said. "I'll be talking to the state police about this conversation, just so you know."

"Give them my love," Thurman said, snorting. "And tonight, when you kiss your wife and kids goodnight, it might be wise to fucking remember that they're only here because of me."

Suddenly, John Pilate's reason evaporated. He balled his fists at his side and flexed his hands, forcing them to relax. "We'll continue this later," Pilate said.

"I'll be around," Thurman said.

* * *

"That *hombre* is a real asshole," Taters said as the pair sped away from the Brown Betty.

"Yeah, he is," Pilate said.

"Did he threaten you, like you half-expected?"

"He showed his hand a bit. Not sure why though. It's not like I used any spectacular feats of investigative legerdemain on him," Pilate said, checking his rearview mirror.

"Whatever that means," Taters said. "Did you like my little tantrum? Oscar-worthy performance, huh?"

"Well played. I appreciate it. It threw him off a bit."

"Good. What's next?"

"Home. I need a drink."

"I'll take some Mexican swill, if you've got any."

* * *

"Derek Krall?" Kate said, her elbows propped on the backyard bar, eyeing her Modelo.

"Can't say I've had the pleasure," Taters said.

Pilate sipped his martini, waving away a gnat that had taken a shine to the wedge of lemon in the glass. "I think she was talking to me. What about Krall?"

"What about him?"

"He was the librarian here at the college. He had a lot to do with dragging me into the whole conspiracy. He played me and Lindstrom and Ollie against each other."

Taters's eyebrows waggled. "Wait. He was the guy who knew where all the bodies were buried?"

"Literally," Kate said.

"Yeah, he nearly got me and Kate killed. He cornered me in the library during the blizzard. If his gun hadn't blown up in his face, I'd probably be fish food in the river right about now."

"Gotcha."

"Anyway, what about him, Kate?" Pilate said.

"Well, when you told me about that tunnel under the Mostek place that leads to Cusack's, it reminded me of something Derek told me once, way before you got to Cross. He took a break from his usual bit of nasty talk to me when I was at the library because he was so excited about something he'd found out about the Mostek place."

"What did he find?"

Kate looked sheepish. "You know what a perv he was. I was trying to get away from him, so I didn't listen for long. I just remember him saying Mostek was sitting on a goldmine without even knowing it."

"Goldmine?" Pilate asked, placing his glass on the bar.

"I thought he meant Mostek was gonna make a ton of money because the other grocery store, the one over on Seventh, had just closed." Kate shrugged. "I thought Krall meant Perry Mostek would have a monopoly on groceries here. I mean, that's true, but what if it was something else? Something literally under the store?"

"Well, we spent a good amount of time under there and came up with zilch, other than a couple old holes in the ground and a musty passage between the two."

"Yeah, hardly a goldmine," Taters offered before another swig of his Modelo.

Kate's brow knitted. "How carefully did you look around down there?"

"Well," Pilate said, "we gave it a pretty solid look, right, Taters?"

"We probably coulda looked a little closer, truth be told."

"What if what was under there is already gone?" Kate said. "Maybe somebody already hauled it outta there."

"Mommy!" Kara called from the back door. "Petey's crying."

"Be right there, sweetie," she called back. "John, what if somebody found something valuable under there and took it?"

"And perhaps that person is now on some pretty nasty shit lists," Taters said.

"And that person is still alive for one reason and one reason only," Pilate said.

"Right. Because he knows where the buried treasure is now," Kate said.

"And Hilmer Thurman isn't about to kill him till he gets it."

Kate took another swig of beer. "Guys, I'd say Parker Nemec is in more trouble than we thought."

"Daddy!" Kara called from the backdoor.

"Honey, your mom is coming," he called over his shoulder.

"No, Daddy, there's a man knocking on the front door. I think he's crying."

Chapter Twenty-Four

Parker Nemec didn't look well. His face was gray, his eyes red and sunken, as if he hadn't slept for days. His hair was a mass of bedhead, his clothing wrinkled and slept in. His right arm was in a tattered sling, immobile, a side effect from the axe attack. Pilate observed that the fingernails on his good arm were chewed to the quick.

Nemec brought the Marlboro light to his lips, leaning on the backyard bar. "She left," he said. The fading sunlight added to Nemec's zombie-like pallor, reminding Pilate of Thurman's stupid remark about doomsday preparation.

"Your wife? Where'd she go?" Pilate asked.

"To her folks, back in Norfork," he said, pronouncing it the Nebraska way.

Taters opened a beer and slid it over to him.

Nemec switched the cigarette to his sling hand and scooped up the small bottle of beer. He took two deep swallows, then pulled his lips back from his gap-toothed grill.

"Why didn't you go with her?" Pilate asked.

Nemec looked at Pilate, his eyes simultaneously hard and tired. "Because he'll come after me, and if I'm with her, she'll get hurt. I gotta fix this here and now."

"Who put that axe in your back, Parker?" Pilate said.

Nemec drank more Modelo. "Tom," he confessed after a gulp. "You know, that fat fuck henchman of Thurman's."

Both men nodded.

"I was trying to talk some sense into Thurman about this whole Mostek thing, and Tom crept up behind me. Son-of-a-bitch that hurt. I mean, I know an axe to the back isn't exactly a hangnail, but I had no idea it would be that much pain."

"How did you get away?"

"That's the funny thing," Nemec said. "I thought I was finished, but then Thurman realized he couldn't finish me off till I told him where it is."

"What? Where what is?"

Nemec swallowed the rest of the beer in two swigs, then placed the empty bottle on the bar. "Nice bar, by the way, Sheriff."

"Close enough," Taters said.

Pilate coaxed, "Answer the question, Parker. What did Thurman nearly killed you over?"

"Let me put it this way," Nemec said. "If I tell you, you'll be as big a target as I am."

"Parker, just tell me, before you get your ass arrested."

"I'm countin' on that," he said. "I want you to arrest me. I want protection. Take me out of town."

"You got it. We'll talk with Commissioner Ryder and the state police and take you to Lincoln."

"That may be tough," Nemec said.

"Why?" Taters barked.

"Because I tried to skip town a few minutes ago, and Tom damn near ran me off the road. I managed to squeeze past him on Cemetery Road. He's parked down the street right now, waiting for me to leave."

"Nice driving for a one-armed man," Pilate said, "and thanks a lot for bringing him to my house, you piece of shit. I have kids in there."

"Sorry, Constable. I had nowhere else to go."

"Let's get inside."

* * *

Pilate hung up the phone. "Well, we have about three or four hours before reinforcements are due to arrive. Ryder says there's a hostage situation at a liquor store over in Vetsville, so all the reserve deputies and state police are over there."

"How convenient," Kate said.

Peter, oblivious, chirped happily, pointing at everyone and cooing as he lay in his mother's protective arms.

Pilate nodded. "Ryder's heading this way though. That's something." He looked at Nemec. "We've gotta get you out of my house." Pilate picked up his gun and holster. "Kate, would you show Taters the gun safe?"

"Yep," she said.

"See? Guns *can* come in handy," Taters said.

She flashed him a dirty look, then smirked and shook her head. "Come on."

"What's so damn important to Thurman and Cusack, Nemec?"

"Oh, you know about Mr. Lucky Charms, eh?" Nemec said, his eyes darting to Pilate's.

"Yes. I'm not a complete idiot," Pilate said.

"He found out by accident," Nemec said.

"I don't have time to find out by accident, so how about you just cut the shit and tell me?"

"I will, as soon as I feel safe."

Taters and Kate walked back downstairs. Taters was holding a hunting rifle and wearing a semiautomatic pistol in his belt. Kate hefted a shotgun.

"Kate, you gonna be okay, hon'?" Pilate said.

"Yep," she said. "There won't be any trouble once you get Mr. Popularity out of here. I know how to use the shotgun…and please don't give me any shit about gun safety right now."

"Where are we going?" Nemec said, pacing on the living room rug.

"Jail," Pilate said.

* * *

"This is not a good idea," Nemec said as Pilate closed the barred door on him.

"Best we can do for the time being," Pilate said. "Now, since you're safely behind bars, tell me what this is all about."

Nemec snorted, falling heavily onto the squeaking springs of the old mattress in the cell. "Shit, I guess it doesn't matter now. You wanna know the whole story?"

Pilate glanced to his right, seeing Taters's shadow in the doorway. "That's the general idea."

"Ever heard of Alvin Blood?"

"Nope. One of those sparkly vampires in those teen girls' books?"

"Hardly. You killed the only guy in town who knew much about him--your old pal, the librarian."

"I didn't kill Derek Krall."

Nemec shrugged. "Krall was researching Al Blood."

Pilate sighed. "So?"

"Derek Krall knew the secret," Nemec said, "or at least he was getting close to figuring it out before all that stuff with Jack Lindstrom and Ollie Olafson went down, right when you moved to town."

"This guy loves the sound of his own voice," Simon said.

"Okay."

Nemec blew a snot rocket on the floor and smudged it with his boot. "Krall knew about the gold, see?"

"Gold?"

"Yeah, the gold buried under Perry Mostek's store and on the old Bartley place and in just about every spot around town that Olafson and Lindstrom were fighting over." He chuckled quietly. "I read your book, John. You got it right in so many ways, but you never really nailed what Lindstrom and Ollie were fighting over. It was Alvin Blood's gold."

"Who the hell is Alvin Blood?"

"A blacksmith back in 1890 or so. Legend has it that ol' Al buried thousands of bucks' worth of gold coins on his property." He gestured with his thumb. "Right across the street."

Pilate shot Taters a look.

"Alvin went to Missouri to buy some merchandise and never returned. The gold was never recovered, and they eventually built a house on top the smithy site. Krall found out in his research that Alvin Blood had an interesting life before becoming a blacksmith. He was apparently a road agent, a pretty good one. He was the terror of the territory," Nemec said.

"But he settled down to blacksmithing, and Krall also figured out it wasn't just his takings but actually some Confederate gold entrusted to him by one Jubal Olafson. Yeah, same family. Now, a prostitute in Fort Kearney killed old Jubal, and Alvin was left to guard the gold. You know what it's worth in today's dollars?"

Pilate shrugged.

"Roughly a million, and that's not all. Krall found out about all this in an old diary supposedly written by Blood's estranged wife. It says he had a few three-dollar Indian Head Princess coins, including an 1855-D one-dollar gold coin. Those coins aren't just pocket change, John. In the right condition, that one coin alone's worth $150,000. That's money worth killing for."

Taters whistled and walked into the back with the two men. "Hell yeah. Let's everybody kill everybody else over less than my life insurance policy."

"You have a million in life insurance?" Pilate said.

"Doesn't everybody?"

"So Jack Lindstrom knew about this?" Pilate asked Nemec.

"Not exactly. Krall was good at stringing him along. All Lindstrom knew was that Ollie wanted something, and Krall made sure Ollie felt like Lindstrom was breathing down his neck."

Pilate sat down on an old wooden chair. "Jesus. People died over this bullshit."

"Not bullshit. It's all about money, power, control. This little town may not be much, but men will fight over money, land, and pussy, no matter how small the stain on the map."

"I see precious little of the latter in all this," Taters said.

"Can't win 'em all."

"To be clear, Hilmer Thurman knows about this?"

Nemec smiled, with little mirth. "He said Ollie talked to him about it before he died. Ollie was considering bringing in some extra muscle to deal with you and former Sheriff Scovill. So, when Ollie got his ticket punched, Thurman hightailed it down here."

"He did move in pretty quick," Pilate mused.

"Ollie caught Krall snooping around Mostek's place, and Krall made a special effort to keep Lindstrom from tearing down the old place Cusack bought and fixed up into the Cross and Cork. Ollie leaned on Krall and got him to tell him what he knew, except--"

"You, in the jail!" interrupted a voice from outside.

"Shit," Taters said, cocking his rifle.

"Wait here, Taters," Pilate said. He hurried to the front door of the jail and peered out through the shutters, but he saw no one.

"Hello? You there, in the cell," the familiar voice called again. "Constable, we just want the banker. Give us Nemec, and nobody gets hurt."

"Except Nemec?" Pilate called.

"Just send him out," the man shouted.

"Don't let them get me!" Nemec called from his cell. "You said I'd be safe."

"Shut up, you," Taters said.

"Whoever you are, you need to get your ass back home or crawl back under whatever rock you came from," Pilate called through an opening in the shutters. "You're dangerously close to committing a crime."

"You gonna send him out or what?"

"No."

"Okay."

The headlights of a massive pickup turned on, flooding the jail with light that crept through cracks in the shutters. The engine roared to life, and the truck sped away.

"Interesting," Simon said. *"You need to piss? 'Cause I sure as hell do."*

"Simon, you're not real. You can't even piss, except to piss me off."

"Were you listening just now, John?"

"John?" Taters said, his face quizzical.

"Never mind. It seems we have a bit of a problem."

"Yeah, I think you pegged that right."

Chapter Twenty-Five

Pilate sipped coffee from a chipped mug, watching Parker Nemec pace in his tiny cell.

"Why are we staying here? Don't you think we should make a break for it?"

Pilate leaned back in the chair, balancing on two legs. "Nope. We set foot outside this jail, and we're due to get shot. Even if we get past them, they'll ambush before we hit the edge of town."

"Aren't you worried about your wife and kids?"

"Nope. As soon as we left my house, I knew we were being followed. I told Kate to tear outta town as soon as the coast was clear. She's on her way to Goss City, to a secure location, as they say—kinda like your wife when she ran off to Norfolk."

Nemec smiled. "Well done, Constable. But what do we do now? Just wait here till they burn the place down?"

"I doubt they'll do that, considering that you're in here, and you're apparently the only one who knows the secret to Curly's gold."

"Blood. Blood's gold," Nemec said.

"Blood's gold doesn't have Jack Palance," Taters said from behind the door of the tiny bathroom, his voice echoing off the walls.

"Good point," Pilate said. "So, Parker…"

"What?"

"Where's the gold? It's not under Cusack's, and I'm not sure he even knows it exists."

"Well, he was leaned on pretty hard by Thurman, so he brought in some Irish muscle, some guy called Jackie the Crow."

"The Crow? That's new. Okay, but where's the gold?"

Nemec smiled. "That's the worst part about all this, John."

"What?"

"I have no idea. I can't find it."

"What do you mean, you can't find it?" Taters asked in disbelief, waving his hands in the air to dry them after walking out of the restroom. "Surely it's in the county budget to buy a new roll of paper towels."

"And air freshener, hopefully," Pilate replied, then turned back to Nemec. "Well?"

"Before all the shit went down, Krall was getting pretty tight over at the Brown Betty. I played poker there with Krall, Robie, and Harley Cordwainer. Krall was pretty pleased with himself, said Perry Mostek was sitting on a goldmine and didn't even know it," Nemec said. "Coffee?"

Pilate poured him a cup and handed it through the bars.

"Thanks. Anyway, he dropped a few vague hints and toddled off. Right after Krall and Ollie ended up dead, and before Perry Mostek went nuts and shot Sheriff Welliver and skipped town, if he really did…" He put the coffee down and scrubbed at his scalp with his good hand in a nervous gesture. "I suspect he ended up dead. Anyway, before Thurman turned up, I managed to sneak in to what's now the Cusack place. Incidentally, it was built on the same spot as the Al Blood blacksmith shop back in the day." Nemec sipped the coffee and made a face. "Ick! I've tasted piss better than this."

"You've tasted piss?" Taters said.

"Well, no, but anyway, I found the trapdoor and went down there. Crept through that horror-movie tunnel to the chamber under Mostek's place and found an old box full of gold coins. It was like a pirate treasure."

"I can imagine," Pilate said.

"I hoisted it all back up through what's now Cusack's place and made tracks."

"Then what?"

"One night, I buried it in a field behind the old Bartley place. It was a bitch to dig deep enough in that frozen soil, but I did it. Before I could figure out my next move, though, we got socked in by that blizzard, you killed Ollie, Krall got what was coming to him, and then I couldn't fucking find where I buried the gold once it all thawed out."

Taters chortled. "You're an idiot. You know that? And to think, people trust you with their life savings. I wouldn't deposit a rolla pennies in that damn bank of yours. You'd probably bury it in a rabbit hole and forget where you put it."

"Screw you, mister," Nemec said.

"You're lying. You know exactly where it is, but you don't want to give it up," Pilate said.

"Yeah, sure. I'm so cocksure of myself that I took an axe blade to the back to keep my stubborn secret." Nemec guffawed. "You're the idiot if you think I didn't tell them there and then that I would give up the gold, but...well..."

"You really couldn't find where you buried it?" Pilate said.

"This is too much," Taters said.

"They can't kill me until they have the gold or are positive that I'm lying and they can sweat it out of me."

"So somewhere in the fields behind the Bartley place, there's a shit-ton of gold?" Pilate said.

"Unless somebody else already found it," Taters said.

Pilate shrugged at Taters. "What side of the place did you bury it? East or west?"

"East, facing town. I do remember that."

"Within view of at least five or six nearby houses," Pilate muttered. "Over by Mrs. Drum's turd-strewn lawn."

A loud banging at the front door interrupted Pilate.

"Stay with him, T."

"You got it," Taters said, gesturing for Nemec to get on the floor.

Pilate carefully edged up the hall to the outer office. Crouching behind his desk, gun drawn, he called out, "Who is it?"

"It's me, Sheriff. Riley, Riley Pierson."

"What are you doing here, Nebraska?"

"I need to talk to you about Abbey. I saw your car out front and--"

Pilate sprang up, peered out the shutters, and opened the door. He grabbed Riley by the collar and jerked him inside.

"Hey!"

"Not safe," Pilate said, quickly locking the door. "Anybody else out there?"

"I dunno. I didn't see anybody," Riley said. "What's up?"

"Well, we have a situation here," Pilate said. "I hate to tell you this, but you're stuck here now. I can't let you back out until help arrives."

"What the heck are you talking about?"

"Kid, can you shoot?" Taters asked from the back room.

"Yeah. I hunt."

"Good. Consider yourself a deputy constable," Pilate said. "My friend Taters back there has a Winchester and a pistol. Pick your favorite, whatever you handle best, and we'll talk."

* * *

"So we got a .38, a semiautomatic pistol, a Winchester '92 rifle, and the varmint gun loaded with birdshot," Pilate said. "Looks like we have about fifty rounds or so apiece."

"Could be worse," Taters said.

"Oh? How?"

"We only need to hole up in here till reinforcements arrive. Didn't Ryder say they'll be here in three or four hours?"

Pilate nodded.

"Well, it's already been an hour, so not much longer."

"True."

Nemec sat up from his recumbent position on the squeaky cot. "Could you let me out and give me a gun?"

"No."

"That just stinks, Sheriff."

"Who is it that wants Mr. Nemec?" Riley asked, rubbing his cheek as he double-checked the lock on the reinforced steel back door of the jail.

"Hilmer Thurman."

"The guy who owns the Brown Betty?"

"The very one."

"Oh."

"C'mon, Nebraska. You handled that old door so well that I want you to help me barricade the front door. The shutters and wooden door can only take so much. We'll use my desk."

They started to push the heavy oak desk toward the door when the *pop-pop-pop* of gunshots pierced the thick air of the jail.

"Well, we're in the thick of it now, boys," Taters hollered. "Anchors away!"

"Everybody stay low!" Pilate shouted, crawling behind the desk with Riley.

More shots tore into the front door and windows of the jail, raining glass and splinters from the shutters into the office.

"Holy shit!" Riley yelled. "Are they trying to kill us?"

"Stay calm," Pilate said. "They're just trying to rattle us."

"Well, it's working."

A louder series of *bangs* rang out as what seemed like a hundred shotgun blasts tore bigger hunks out of the door, windows, and the shutters behind them.

"Okay, John, I don't think that's rattling. Ready or not, here they come," Simon said.

Pilate looked at Riley. "Looks like we're not gonna be able to just wait them out. We have to fight back."

Riley nodded, his hands shaking visibly as he cradled the Winchester '92.

"When I count to three, hop up and fire two shots through the hole in the window. You got it?"

"Okay," Riley said, cocking the rifle.

"Don't worry about aiming. We've just gotta give them something to think about, make a little noise. Okay. One, two, three!"

Pilate and Riley rose up and fired two shots each through the hole in the ravaged window and shutters, their rounds flying off into the night. The smell of spent cartridges hung in the air, coupled with a think layer of smoke.

"You okay?"

"Yeah," Riley said. "I just...well, I just wish I coulda seen Abbey one more time."

"Don't talk like that, Riley. We're gonna get outta here just fine."

"No, that's not what I mean."

"What do you mean?"

"She wouldn't see me at the hospital," he said.

"Well, you can see her tomorrow," Pilate said.

"Promise?" Riley's hands shook again.

Taters crawled up between them. "How we doing?"

"Well, they're turning the front of the building to Swiss cheese, but I think we put a scare in 'em with my trusty .38 and Nebraska's '92."

"I bet you're right," Taters said, "but we've got another issue to contend with."

"What?"

"Somebody's pounding on the back door."

Chapter Twenty-Six

The ringing of the telephone pierced the chaos; somehow, it had survived the onslaught and was still sitting in its place on the heavy desk.

Pilate reached for it. "That all you got?" he said, amping up the bravado.

"Open the goddamn door," a man's voice ordered.

"Um…no. I figured our response to your shotguns was a good enough--"

"Pilate, you dumbass, it's me, Ryder. I'm at the back door. I dropped one of those bastards to get back here, but if you don't hurry and let me in by the hair of my damn chinny-chin-chin, they're gonna catch on. Open the fucking door! That's an order, Constable!"

"Taters, get back there. It's Ryder!"

Taters crawfished back to the door and swiftly opened it to let Ryder in, then hurriedly locked the door again.

While he was usually laconic, with not a hair out of place, Ryder looked distinctly ruffled: his cowboy hat was slightly askew.

Pilate told Riley to watch the door. "Shoot at anything that tries to come in," he said, then crawled back to the cell area. "Well, this is certainly one fucked-up state of affairs," Pilate said, trying hard to smile. "Damn fine way to earn a grand a month."

"Well, sometimes you get the bear, sometimes the bear gets you," Ryder said, checking the chambers of his Colt New Frontier pistol. "What do we have here?"

"Well, Mr. Nemec, here, is in protective custody, though he's confessed to being an accessory to a whole lotta bullshit."

"Hey! I have immunity!" Nemec said, hands on the bars.

"Whatever," Pilate said, keeping his eyes on Ryder. "Taters and Riley Pierson are deputies."

"A civilian boat jockey and a kid?" Ryder asked, looking cockeyed at Pilate. "That's all you got?"

"Yup. The kid showed up before things got hairy. Couldn't risk sending him out, so Nebraska stays," Pilate said.

"Good thinking," Ryder said.

"My wife--"

Ryder shook his head. "Sorry, pal, but Kate and the kids couldn't get out. I got a call from dispatch on the way over. She tried to call here, but couldn't get through. She's gone underground."

"Damn it! I have to go get her."

"You have no idea where she is, and we can't make a move without those trigger-happy fools seeing it," Ryder said. "The best thing you can do for yourself and your missus is to take care of business here. I doubt very seriously that Thurman would send any of his goons after her, especially since he's spread pretty thin, trying to draw our people away from town."

"Let's pray you're right. When do we get reinforcements?"

Ryder smiled. "Well, for the time being, you're lookin' at all the reinforcements you're gonna get."

"Well, ain't that just grand?" Taters said. "No offense, but we were hopin' for a SWAT team or something."

"None taken. Me, too, but that liquor store hostage sitch drew the law over to that side of the county. I put a call in to Lew Hawkins, next county over, to see if he could send some fellas this way," Ryder said. "He said he will as soon as they secure some problem over at the airport. Bob Hayes called him and said somebody blew up a Cessna and was taking shots at the tower."

"Shit. They really planned this out," Pilate said.

"Yeah, well, our Mr. Thurman is nothing if not thorough," Ryder said. "Damn. I was afraid of this once I got in. Ready for another kick in the pants?" he asked, holding up his cell phone.

"What?" Pilate patted his pockets for his phone and checked it. "No service."

"They clipped the wires at the tower at Monticello Cemetery, I suspect. That fence ain't all that high," Ryder said.

"Crap. Well, that means his folks can't talk to each other either, and our landline still works."

"Only 'cause they want it to. You can bet they're monitoring it and will cut it off if we try to call for help."

"I'm gonna die, in a gol-damn antique jail cell," Nemec whispered, falling heavily back on his bunk.

"Shut up," Pilate snapped. "Well, what do we do?" he asked, turning back to Ryder.

Ryder holstered his Colt. "We batten down the hatches. 'Bout all we can do at the moment."

"Hold 'em off till the reinforcements get here or sunrise, whichever comes first?" Taters asked.

Ryder nodded, adjusting his hat. "Gimme a rundown on weapons and ammo."

Pilate ran down the list of weaponry and ammo at their disposal.

"Goody. Well, I have Mabel here," he said, patting his Colt, "and about thirty rounds left. I also have this peashooter I took off the guy I clocked out back." He proudly displayed the pilfered .38.

"Nice," Pilate said.

"Yeah. It's got eight rounds, but you have extra here," he said. "Oh yeah, and I also have a surprise in my boot, should we--"

"Mr. Pilate, you'd better get up here!" Riley called.

"C'mon, Commish," Pilate said. "Taters, hang back."

"Yeah, yeah. Babysit the prisoner. Jeez, I feel like Walter Brennan. That's the Taters Malley theory on that."

Pilate nodded at him.

Taters gave him a sign to hang back as Ryder went ahead. "Dude, I know this Ryder used to be in law enforcement and all, but is he as good as he used to be?" he whispered.

"I suspect pretty close," Pilate said, talking low, "though I'd hate to bet my life on the difference."

"Just be careful," Taters said.

"Always."

"A lie if I ever heard one."

Pilate nodded and smiled, then joined Riley and Ryder behind the desk. "What's up?" he asked.

"I saw headlights coming and going," Riley said. "Can't tell if there are more guys or if some of the others just left."

"I'd put money on the former," Ryder said. "Did you get a look at anybody before?"

"Nope, but by the sound of his voice, I'm pretty sure Hilmer's fat-ass toady, Tom, was out there."

"Yeah, Hils ain't gonna be out there in person," Ryder said. "He ain't got the balls for it, just lives vicariously through his brainless sheep. Never gets his hands dirty. That's why we've never been able to lay a glove on him."

"Well, surely we can trace something back to him after this."

"Assuming we survive, we're gonna try to do that very thing, Constable, but we gotta get out alive first."

"Are we gonna make it?" Riley asked.

"No," Simon intoned in Pilate's skull.

"Yes, of course," Pilate contradicted, nudging Ryder.

"Shit, boy, I ain't gonna sugarcoat it. We may not, but even if we don't, I plan to go out like a man, on my feet."

"I don't want to die," Riley said. "I still have to make things right with Abbey."

"Then I'd say you need to avoid dying, boy," Ryder said, patting him on the shoulder.

"I have a name." Riley said.

Ryder nodded. "Sorry, Nebraska."

"Tell me again why the hell we still live here," Simon drawled.

* * *

"Gold? The lost Alvin Blood mother lode?" Ryder cackled, sitting with his boots up on the rickety card table by the jail cell.

"Laugh all you want," Nemec said. "It's real. If it weren't, do you think we'd be in this kind of trouble?"

Ryder shook his head, poking up his hat, revealing a glint of humor in his steely eyes. "Nope. I just never took Derek Krall seriously. I guess I learned my lesson though. He was an evil little shit but a *smart* evil little shit."

The phone rang.

Riley froze, staring at it. "Do I answer?"

"No. Let me," Ryder said, hurrying to the overturned desk. He cracked his knuckles and picked up the old black receiver. "Welcome to Jack Burger. Jack speaking."

"Pilate?" said the man from before.

"No, Tom, this is Ryder."

"Oh." The man sounded startled, though Ryder couldn't discern if it was because he had answered or because he had called Tom by name.

"Tom?"

"Um…that's not my name."

"Tom." Ryder rolled his eyes.

A pause ensued, but it didn't linger long.

"One more time. Tom?"

"For the sake of hurrying the fuck up, you can call me 'Tom'."

"Thanks. Better than 'Dick' or 'Harry'…or 'Hairy Dick,'" Ryder mocked, nodding at Pilate, who had crawled up behind him. "Now look, Tom, you boys need to pack it in before those short-tempered State Patrol boys and every deputy in a fifty-mile radius show up and crawl right up your fat ass."

Tom laughed, albeit nervously. "Nice try, Commissioner, but there ain't any deputies or troopers coming to your aid anytime soon. They're all quite busy with more important matters."

"Yeah, yeah, I know," Ryder drawled. "Your equally half-witted *compadres* have been busy starting fires all over the county."

Pilate eyed Ryder.

"*That guy is the real deal, I must say,*" Simon said, to which Pilate mentally agreed.

"Commissioner, just give us Nemec, and we'll call it a draw. What do you say?"

"Tom," Ryder said, raising his voice an octave so the petrified banker could hear, "you know I'd generally be happy to hand that jackass Nemec over to you--"

"Hey!" Nemec called out.

"But that would probably sign our death warrants, as well as his. You and I both know we'll all be dead two seconds after we shove his big butt out the door, and you'll kill Parker as soon as you get what the kids call the four-one-one outta him. So, no, I don't think we'll take what's behind Door Number One, Monty."

"Huh?"

"Damn it, Tom. Try to keep up, would ya? I know you're not a college grad, but--"

"Shut up! You got ten minutes to send him out, or we'll come in there and get him. He and I have some things to discuss."

"Did you just tell me to shut up?" Ryder said, the timbre of his voice that of the proverbial doornail.

"I, uh…well, you know," Tom stammered. "You know who you're dealing with, and he don't like that kinda talk."

"*He* don't like? Pssh. Let's get this straight, buddy boy. There are a whole lotta damn things I don't like around here. For starters, I don't like your boss's men sittin' on the road like vultures, bottling up this town, blowing up airplanes, and starting shit far away to draw off our allies. I don't like your men watching us, trying to catch us with our backs turned, and I don't like your boss, Hilmer Thurman, because he set all this bullshit up. Furthermore, for the record, I'm not much fond of you."

"Ten minutes," Tom said, then hung up.

"Well, that was refreshingly predictable," Ryder said, handing the receiver to Riley.

"What did he say?"

"They're coming to crash our party in ten minutes if we don't send Parker out there with a rose in his teeth."

"Great."

"Yeah, well, we can file that one under 'ain't happening,' Constable."

"Then what do we do?" Riley said.

"We get ready to reenact Custer's last stand, Nebraska."

Chapter Twenty-Seven

"We don't have a lot of choices here," Pilate said to the men gathered around the cell; Riley was still up front, but he could hear. "We can give up and die, or we can fight it out and probably die."

"Gimme a gun," Nemec said. "Let me help. I deserve a chance to fight for my own life."

Pilate looked at Ryder.

The commissioner looked impassive a moment, then nodded.

"Taters, let him out," Pilate said. "Even with one good arm, he's still another gun in the fight."

Nemec walked out of the cell and accepted the newly acquired .38 from Ryder. "Thank you."

"That gun gets pointed at anybody but a bad guy, and I'll make a personal deposit of two shells in your damn balls," Taters said.

"I like this guy," Ryder said, jerking a thumb at Taters.

"So what's the plan?" Nemec said, ignoring the threat.

"We divide up and position ourselves in front and back here. They'll do what they're doing out in the county, attack on multiple fronts at once."

"Shit," Pilate said.

"Taters, you and Nemec guard the back door. It's reinforced steel, but they could still break it down or punch holes in it with explosives."

"Charming," Taters said.

"Get behind the cell bunk for cover," Ryder instructed. "Pilate, you and the kid take the front door. Stay behind Ollie's old desk. That heavy-duty relic will stop a lot of their fire."

"What about you, Mr. Commissioner?" Riley asked nervously.

"I don't like to sit still. I'll be a floater."

"Okay," Pilate said.

"Here's the standing order, men," Ryder said, raising his index finger. "We got one rule. Don't shoot till they break down a door. There's no return-on-investment in shooting holes in our own doors and windows. You understand that, don't ya, Mr. Banker?"

Nemec nodded.

"So…don't shoot until we see the whites of their eyes?" Taters murmured, wiping sweat from his brow.

"Exactly," Ryder said.

"You okay, Taters?" Pilate asked.

"I'm fine," he said, a tone of finality in his voice. "Don't wet nurse me, John. Next thing I know, you'll be walkin' around here in a tight white mini-dress with a red cross on it, and none of us wanna see that."

"Sorry."

"I just wish I had a damn Modelo or two."

"Easy there, *borrachón*," Pilate said, smiling.

Taters nodded and managed a brief smile, then again mopped his brow with his sleeve.

"Gents, we have weapons, defensible positions, and ammo to survive this," Ryder said, glancing at his watch. "It's eleven forty p.m. We gotta run out the clock till we get some help or sunrise breaks. I'm confident we can do this," he said, with all the fervor of a football coach before the last quarter of a tie game.

"What's so special about sunrise?" Nemec asked.

"Darkness obscures a multitude of sins, and there's no damn way they'll let themselves be visually identified. They'll pack it in as soon as their guys on the edge of town walkie-talkie over to tell 'em the state cops and deputies are coming. Barring that, we've got the sunrise on our side."

"You don't think they'll engage the troopers?"

"Doubt it," Ryder said, slipping a stick of Wrigley's spearmint between his thin lips. "Though they've already engaged a town constable and county commissioner, so who knows? All bets may be off, though this is already starting to look reckless, something Hilmer usually doesn't do."

"First time for everything," Pilate said. "He's not infallible."

Ryder winked at Pilate. "Look, fellas, there's one more thing. They may also decide that their whole mission is fucked, and they might go kamikaze on us, willing to cut their losses."

"Meaning?" Pilate said.

"They firebomb our little Alamo and roast us all alive."

"Damn. I love this man's optimism," Simon quipped.

* * *

"I never told Abbey I love her," Riley said, his voice barely above a whisper.

Pilate sat with him, shoulder to shoulder, their backs against the overturned desk. "Me neither," Pilate said.

Riley's head jerked upward at Pilate, who broke into a broad grin. "She had such a crush on you," he said, smiling back.

"Yeah, well, I'm flattered. She's a great gal."

"Did you like, uh…you know, like her back? I mean, before things got serious with Miss Nathaniel, did you crush on her?" His eyes were wide, plaintive.

"No, Riley. I care about her very much, but I never crushed on Abbey," Pilate said. "Now, that's not to say I don't find her extremely attractive. Any man would. She's got a lot going for her, as you well know."

"Yeah, but you said it's still okay for me to move on," Riley said.

"Not in so many words," Pilate said. "I only meant you should move on if you don't really love her. That's only fair to both of you."

He nodded. "I think I love her. I mean, I wanna be with her."

"Then let's get out of this shit storm alive so you can march right up to that hospital and tell her."

"I'm gonna go home first," he said.

"What for? A shower?"

"No. I want to get my grandma's ring."

Pilate nodded. "Sweet. Good man."

"Psst, John," Ryder said, peering out a hole in the wooden shutters on the front of the office.

"What?" Pilate whispered.

"I see 'em. They're staging up across the street, in front of Mostek's store. Looks like at least seven or eight guys."

"Thurman?"

He shook his head. "No, but the Hitchockian profile and trucker cap are dead giveaways for Tom."

"What are they doing?" Riley said.

"Hmm," Ryder said. "Looks like they're lining up behind a couple trucks, rifles at the ready."

"So...a firing line?" Pilate inquired.

"I s'pose," Ryder said, drawing his Colt. "Oh my, how predictable."

"What?"

A barrage of gunfire slammed into the door of the jail, sending splinters and debris flying into the desk.

Ryder yelled something unintelligible at the men, then poked the Colt through the hole and fired twice.

"What the hell?" Nemec called from the back.

"Shut up, Park--" Pilate started.

Ryder barked over his shoulder, "That fella tried to deliver a cocktail, but he's sleeping now."

A commotion of voices filtered, and a sudden flash of light illuminated through the walls.

"What?" Pilate said.

Ryder gestured for him to come up.

Pilate crawled up to Ryder and peered outside. A man lay in the middle of the street, motionless and on fire. "Oh my God," Pilate said.

"That was Otis, I'm pretty sure." Ryder clicked his tongue. "Shoulda stuck to playin' lumberjack. I'm just sorry it took two shots to start the fire."

A loud sound from the back of the jail startled them.

"What the hell?" Pilate said.

"Looks like we've got company at the back door," Ryder guessed. "C'mon." Instead of crawling, Ryder ran, upright. "Kid, keep an eye on the front."

Pilate quickly followed the surprisingly agile commissioner.

Nemec shouted and fired two shots into the steel door.

Ryder smacked him on the head. "Stop shootin', damn it! There was one rule!"

The smell of gasoline and smoke crept into the jail.

"Shit. They dropped one of those in the alley," Pilate said. "What do we do?"

"Nothing at the moment," Ryder said. "The alley's closed off. Not much wind back there, so it may burn itself out--"

Ryder was interrupted by a loud moan from Taters.

"Taters?" Pilate said, rushing to catch his friend as he crumpled, dropping his weapon and clutching his chest.

* * *

Pilate and Nemec carried the wilted fisherman behind the bunk and placed a well-worn pillow under his head.

"Taters? You with us?"

His eyes fluttered, and his hand flexed on his chest. "Yeah," he gasped out. "Felt like somebody punched me in the chest just now."

"Have you felt that before?" Nemec said.

"Taters," Pilate said, "is it like before?"

He nodded, quicker this time, and gestured at his shirt pocket.

Pilate put his hand in the shirt pocket. "Nitroglycerin pills? How many?"

Taters extended his index finger.

Pilate placed a pill under Taters's tongue.

Taters's face started to relax almost instantly.

"Take it easy, pal," Pilate said, coughing from the haze of black smoke infiltrating the room.

Taters's eyes fluttered again. "I'm okay, John. Prop me up and let me--"

"No, Taters. We'll take it from here. You just take it easy and rest up for a minute. That's a direct order, Deputy."

"Gee. All that power's gone to your head," he snarked weakly.

Pilate nodded, smiling.

Ryder leaned into the cell. "How's he doing?"

"Better," Pilate said.

Nemec coughed. "Yeah, but we're all gonna asphyxiate in here. Game over, man. Game over."

"Just stay frosty," Pilate said.

"Movie quotes? At a time like this? Frankly, John, they don't give a damn," Simon said.

"Nemec, take the bed sheets and soak 'em in the toilet, then put 'em by against the door. Maybe we can take the smoke down a notch."

Nemec obeyed and went to his task.

"Mr. Pilate!" Riley yelled. "John?"

"Great. Taters?" He searched his friend's face for assent to move.

"Go on," Taters mouthed.

Ryder and Pilate moved to the desk up front and found Riley was at the window. "What?" Pilate said.

"They're lining up again," the kid said. "That guy is still a human candle, but they're just ignoring him and lining up to fire again."

"Looks like they have a few AR-15s," Ryder said to Pilate.

"God, please tell me that's not another word for a grenade launcher."

Ryder shook his head. "Ever heard of M-16s?"

"Yeah. Like in Vietnam, right?"

"Uh-huh," Ryder said. "Well, they have the civvie version, and a couple shotguns. All it's gonna take is a concentrated period of firing on us before the whole place falls down around us."

"What are our options?"

"I'd say we don't have any good ones," Ryder said, double-checking his Colt. "We just sit here and take it unless they try to get in. Won't do no good shooting back, I'd say."

"That sucks."

"Yeah, it sure does."

"Riley, get back here," Pilate said.

"Let me shoot, just once," he said.

"What?"

"If we aren't gonna make it, I want a shot at them before I die," he said.

Pilate looked at Ryder.

Ryder shrugged. "Kid's right. Maybe we should just start firing back. What the hell?"

"It beats lying down, and I don't hear any sirens coming to the rescue."

"It's midnight, kinda like a dark *High Noon*." Ryder smirked.

Pilate nodded.

"Go tell Nemec and Taters we're gonna stir some shit up," Ryder said. "I'll count to ten before I start, so hurry back."

Pilate ran back to Taters and Nemec.

The smoke had cut down considerably after Nemec put the wet sheets by the door. Taters was sitting up and almost looked normal.

"You okay, buddy?"

"Much better. Just a little vagina."

"Vagina? Don't you mean angina?"

"I prefer the former to the latter. Whatever," Taters said. "What's the plan?"

"We're outgunned, pal. We aren't gonna make it."

"Well, shit. Jordan's gonna be pissed at you for getting me killed."

"Is that the Taters Malley theory on that?"

The men chuckled.

"We plan to go out in a blaze of glory. You in?"

"Hell yeah! Wouldn't have it any other way," Taters said. "Help me up and gimme my gun. If I'm gonna die in this two-bit town, rather than under a surgeon's saw, I'm damn well taking some of those pricks with me."

"Parker, we're going up front. Stay back here and shoot anything that moves."

Nemec looked at Pilate, incredulous. "With four bullets?"

"You shouldn't have wasted those two before."

"You're an asshole," Nemec said.

"Shut the hell up," Taters said, "and get behind this mattress."

Taters and Pilate edged to the front, where Ryder had positioned himself to the right of the shuttered front window.

Riley was behind the desk, his rifle resting on the edge and pointing at the door.

"Go get Parker," Ryder said from beneath the brim of his hat.

"Why?" Pilate asked.

"Just get him."

Riley shrugged and went to fetch the banker.

"Okay, fellas, now here's how's it's gonna go down," Ryder said. "We're gonna take the offensive advantage. I'm gonna run out the door. I've got Mabel and her little brother, Walter." He produced a small pistol from his boot; the weapon resembled the Walther PPK Sean Connery brandished as James Bond. "I'm gonna let them make their displeasure known, and you guys are gonna run out behind me. Parker, you still have your key to the bank?"

"Yeah," he said, confused.

"We'll cover you while you unlock the door. Y'all scramble in there and lock yourselves in the vault."

"That's crazy, man," Pilate said. "You'll be killed."

Ryder looked pained. "I have no intention of dying today, Constable. I think if we surprise 'em, throw some lead on the fly, it'll throw them off their game. They'll have a tough time seeing us in the dark, and we might just pull it off."

"What if they turn on the floodlights on their trucks?" Riley asked.

Ryder shrugged again. "Then we die in the limelight, just like I've always wanted."

Taters clapped Pilate on the shoulder. "It just might work."

"Can you run?"

"Shit fire, man, it's not a matter of can. It's a matter of have to."

"I'd say they're gearing up," Ryder said, peering out the window. "We'd better hit it. Everybody locked and loaded, as they say in the movies?"

"I think I just loaded my pants," Riley said.

"Me too," Nemec said.

"C'mon, Parker. Getting shot can't possibly hurt as bad as an axe in your back."

"That is a theory I don't want to test," Nemec said.

"John, it's been lovely," Simon said.

Chapter Twenty-Eight

Pilate's thoughts flashed to the faces of Kate, Kara, and Peter. *I wish I could hold my little boy and kiss my girls one more time.*

Ryder looked at his ostrich boots. "Ya know, I love these, but they're a royal bitch to run in."

"These too," Pilate said, looking at his own footwear.

"Everybody got your track shoes on?" Ryder said, launching a speck of spittle beside him. "Sorry, Parker. You got your high heels on and pantyhose hitched up?"

"Ha-ha," he said, his voice trembling, causing each syllable to stretch into two.

Pilate released one of his long, drawn-out sighs, trying to relieve his nerves.

"Anybody wanna say a prayer?" Riley said.

"Yeah, but I'm outta spit," Taters said. "I need a--"

"Modelo? Yeah, we know, *borrachón*," Pilate said.

"John, one thing…"

Pilate nodded.

"Shane lived."

"Yeah, yeah."

"Say it. Say it now," Taters said, without a hint of humor.

"What's he yapping about?" Nemec said.

Ryder smiled. "I think I get it."

"You win, Taters. Shane lived. Of course he did."

"Liar," Simon said.

"Yeah, I feel better already," Taters said, cocking his weapon. "Hey, maybe we'll get a pretty lady to throw a flower pot through the window for us as a distraction."

"Nebraska, go for the prayer."

Riley bowed his head. "Lord, let us live." He looked up.

"That's it?" Ryder said. "No thees and thous or daily bread or valley of the shadow of death or anything?"

"That's all I got."

"I like it. I'm sure even God can appreciate a little Hemingway now and then," Pilate said. He swallowed hard, fighting the urge to throw up, which was odd because he couldn't even remember the last thing he'd eaten.

"Okay. Well, here we go." Ryder looked outside. "You guys unlock the door and get ready. When I give the go-ahead, open the door and get the hell outta my way. You don't wanna get on Mabel's bad side. She's not too picky when she gets to naggin'."

"I'll go next and lay down some cover fire for Nebraska, then Taters and finally Parker," Pilate said. "Parker, as soon as you're out the door, hustle over to the bank door and unlock it."

"Wait," Nemec said. "I only have one good hand. Maybe I should help lay down fire and let the kid run over and unlock the door."

"Good safety tip, Egon. Let's do that," Pilate said.

Nemec handed Riley the key.

"What about the door code?" he asked.

"Are you kidding?" Nemec said.

* * *

"Now!" Ryder bellowed.

Pilate practically ripped the wounded door off its hinges, making a hole for Ryder, who was through in half a second. He dropped to one knee behind a large clay planter and started to fire Mabel and Walter the Walther at the line of men across the street.

Standing to Ryder's left, Pilate fired his Smith & Wesson. Out of the corner of his eye, he saw Taters and Riley pass him, making a panicked beeline for the bank. Nemec ran behind them for a few steps, then stopped and raised his pistol to fire.

"Damn it, Parker, don't play hero! Just run!" Pilate screamed as he fired into the stunned group.

A shot fired from behind the truck and whizzed past Pilate's ear. The *pop* of several rifles warned him that the surprise element was now mercilessly over.

"Oomph," Nemec said, clutching his belly and falling down.

"Goddamn it," Ryder said, emptying Mabel and Walter. He dropped the smaller gun and reached for a speed-loader to feed Mabel.

Pilate crouched and tapped Ryder on the shoulder. "C'mon, Commish. Help me get him up!"

"Just go, John," Ryder said, snapping the cylinder back and aiming.

A series of *pops* caught Ryder, dropping him flat on his back.

"Shit," Pilate said, looking from Ryder to Nemec to Taters and Riley.

"John, come on!" Taters called from the door. "We're in!"

"Man down! I can't leave them," Pilate said. He emptied his weapon into the group across the street and started to sling Ryder over his shoulder.

"I'm okay," Ryder said. "Just a couple stingers. Help me up, and let's go."

More *pops* went off, and Pilate dropped to the ground, hiding behind the swiftly disintegrating planter. He covered his head with his hands.

"We're done," Ryder said.

"By God, you're not gonna do this to me!" Taters yelled, firing his shotgun and moving toward the three men.

"No, Taters! Just go!" Pilate tried to yell above the blasts.

"What the…?" Ryder said, poking Pilate's arm and pointing across the street. "They're firing behind them!"

Pilate poked his head up and saw the muzzle flash of rifles firing toward Mostek's storefront. "Oh my God. There's somebody shooting at them from Mostek's!"

Three more rifle shots rang out, only to be answered by four shotgun blasts from the store. Then, as if someone had pulled the plug on the whole tumultuous outbreak, silence claimed the street.

Ryder pulled himself up with one arm, the other pushing on a wound in his upper right chest. Pilate steadied him and helped him to his feet.

"Parker, can you walk?" Taters asked behind them.

"Think so," Nemec said. "What happened?"

"I have no idea," Pilate said.

The moon peeked out from behind the clouds, revealing several motionless bodies scattered around the trucks.

"Hello, in the jail!" a voice with a familiar lilt called.

"Cusack?" Pilate said.

"I thought maybe you could use a wee bit of help," Cusack said, stepping out of Mostek's store.

"You mean we," another Irish voice said from behind Cusack. The man lit a cigarette, briefly illuminating his smile.

"Fair enough. Gents, meet Jackie the Crow."

"I fookin' love a good gunfight," Jackie said. "Anybody care for a fag?" he said, holding up his pack.

"And they say God protects fools and Irishmen," Ryder said. "Maybe they need to change that."

"I agree," said Kate, stepping out from behind the men, holding a smoking shotgun.

"Kate?" Pilate said.

"Don't look at me that way. I wasn't about to sit idly by and let those bastards slaughter you. It's my job to keep you safe."

"That's a helluva pot through the window," Taters laughed.

Pilate exhaled, as if for the first time in days, ran to his wife, and pulled her into a tight embrace. "Honey, I think it's time you get some cowgirl boots."

"I think you're right," she said.

"Where are the kids?"

"Our babies are safe and sound, John, with Marcy at the Cross and Cork."

"I didn't know you ran a nursery, too, Cusack...but thank you," Pilate said.

"Think nothin' of it," he said softly, glancing back at Jackie the Crow.

Jackie puffed on his cigarette and looked up at the moon, then whistled a few bars of "Raglan Road".

"Well then, the only family casualty was the Saab," Taters said, pointing to the car parked in front of the bank. It was riddled with holes from shotgun and rifle ammunition, all four tires flat.

"Crap," Pilate said. "I hardly knew her."

* * *

"I always miss all the fun," Trooper Hulsey complained, hands on his hips.

"Sounds like you had some fun of your own at the edge of town," Pilate offered.

"Meh, those cowards dropped their weapons as soon as we rolled up. And before you ask, they're out-of-towners, smalltime thugs from up Minnesota way."

"Shocker." Pilate waved as Burl Crites loaded Nemec and Ryder into the ambulance.

Nemec called to Pilate, "Just for the record, this hurts worse than the axe."

"Burl, how they doing?"

"Parker needs surgery, but I'd say he'll be okay," he said, moving quickly to get in the driver's seat. "Ryder's got a bullet in his upper right chest. We'll have to dig it out."

"I'm fine," Ryder called. "Just take care of the crime scene, Constable."

"Will do, Commissioner."

Pilate looked at Taters. "You should get to the hospital, too, don't you think?"

"Nah. I got my magic pills, and I'll be right as rain."

"Bullshit...but you do look okay," Pilate said. "I can't believe we made it outta there alive."

"I dunno. It's not like they were pirates or anything."

"True."

"Mr. Pilate, I'll see you at the hospital in a few."

"You hurt, Nebraska?" Taters asked.

"No," Pilate said, nodding at Riley. "He just needs to get to the hospital, right after he makes a stop at home." Pilate shook Riley's hand. "You did great back there, kid."

"Thanks John. Just keeping it level."

Taters watched the troopers as they placed the dead bodies in bags. "We need to go arrest that sum-bitch Thurman."

"We do," Pilate said, "but not now."

"What the hell do you mean?"

"We got dead bodies here. Tom's dead, his guts sprayed all over the side of his truck. Otis is a pile of barbecue, and that's his pal Bart Robeson over there, or at least a good portion of 'im. Not one of these bodies tells us anything that proves Thurman was behind this."

"Well, what about the fellas they caught on the edge of town?"

"They'll be questioned, but Thurman's placed many layers between himself and them. Same, I'm sure, for the guys who attacked the airport and the ones who took hostages at the liquor store."

"How the hell do we catch the bastard then?" Taters said.

"We have to start outthinking the guy. He's weak now, and we have to use that advantage to trip him up."

"That's all we got? A little temporary leverage while he licks his wounds? That sucks," Taters said.

"Best we can do right now. We have to do it by the book."

"What about Cusack and that Hawk fella?"

"Crow," Pilate corrected with a smile. "I'm sure as shit not pressing charges on him," Pilate said. "If I do, I have to arrest Kate too."

"Yeah, I can see how putting your little lady in handcuffs would be a problem…or maybe not," Taters said with a naughty grin.

"Stop."

"Okay. Well, what now?"

"Now, we go get my wife and kids and book a trip back to Key West," Pilate said. "I have another book to write, and you need to get that ticker fixed and get that boat wet."

"True, but what about that?" Taters asked, tapping Pilate's badge with his finger.

"I'll give it back," Pilate said. "I'm a writer, not a sheriff."

"Constable."

"Close enough."

Mrs. Drum walked through the police line, wearing a housecoat, slippers, and curlers in her gray hair, seemingly oblivious to the carnage around her. "Sheriff!"

"Mrs. Drum," Pilate said, "you really shouldn't be here. This is no place for a--"

"Are you *ever* gonna catch the boy who keeps pooping on my lawn?"

Pilate looked at Taters. "See? If I can't crack the Case of the Creeping Crapper, what business do I have in law enforcement anyway?"

* * *

The moon retreated behind the clouds, obscuring a man wearing a pair of fuzzy slippers, cartoonish spectacles, and a bathrobe. He squatted on Mrs. Drum's lawn and let out a grunt. "How sweet it is," he said.

Once he was finished, he wiped himself, and put the tissue in a plastic bag. He walked back to his home, went inside, and locked the door behind him.

"My precious," Harley Cordwainer said, rubbing his hands together and giggling as he hovered over a card table in the corner of his living room, a wobbling thing, straining under the weight of hundreds of gold coins.

end

JOHN PILATE WILL RETURN
IN
Pilate's Seven

Afterword

Writing is a solitary effort, but publishing is not.

I had not planned on writing another John Pilate book, but I kept hearing voices in the oddest places…

Minding my own business on social media, I'd see that Pilate convinced a Twitter buddy like @Zoofster to ask when the next book was coming. I'd be at my kid's school and a teacher would say she "sure could use another Pilate story" (had to be Kate pulling those strings). My colleagues at work--no doubt put up to it by that snarky Simon--would imply I'd given up on Pilate and Co. too soon. Heck, even my old school chums were clamoring for another adventure with our neurotic hero John and his pal Taters.

I realized I missed Pilate, his friends…and enemies, too.

So, here he is…fulfilling the prophecy about blood…all because of you, my friends, family, fellow authors and perhaps sweetest of all, anonymous readers of mystery thrillers who dare to read stuff that isn't on the bestseller lists, *thank you.*

Special thanks to these folks--you all helped me so much--in ways you'll probably never understand (in no particular order): Michael Zuffa (the aforementioned @Zoofster), Pam Sankey, Jason Gertzen, Noah Smith (great tagline!), Kathleen Weatherby, Harvey Hurtt, Alee Reed (Nelda's biggest fan), Eddie Mann, Colin Hay, Grace and Paul Medina, Neil Finn, Brian and Tammy Hutton, real-life Frontdoor Backyard Bar sages Dave McBrayer and Tony Holland, Erica Tucker, Ryan and Kristin Long, Jeff and Wanda Hamilton, Aimee' Walker, the REAL LIVE John Pilate (finish your book, John!), Bruce Rodgers, Jason C. McIntyre, Deb Trivitt, John Edmondson, Catherine Goodson, James Sudik, and my Dad, Alexander F. Greenwood (I can't believe you finally read the books). Mom, too!

Sharon and Mick Donoff, thanks for letting me hang out and write a few chapters at your beautiful beach house.

My apologies if I left anyone out--it wasn't intentional.

Special thanks to my longtime beta reader, Barb Harris for her humor, support and sharp eyes.

To my talented new book cover artist Scarlett Rugers, thanks for making the series look "big time"!

Autumn Conley, your editing is inspired. Welcome back to the John Pilate Mystery Series. (Hire Autumn if you need a superb editor: autiej@gmail.com)

Thanks to David, Adriane and all the folks at Lulu who put up with my grouchiness.

Author and online guru Michelle Stinson Ross worked her butt off promoting this book. She is so creative and smart about the whole Internet thing. Thank you, my friend.

Eden Baylee deserves some form of sainthood for her encouragement and friendship, but all I can confer upon her is the title of Most Generous and Encouraging Author in North America, if not the world. Please read her books--especially her new mystery series--she's at EdenBaylee.com.

Eden and my pal Mike Hulsey saved this book. I very nearly quit in the middle. It would not be here without their help. True story.

Thanks to the late Robert E. Trevathan, John Wayne, Howard Hawks and Leigh Brackett--I borrowed a little inspiration from you all for this one. You are missed.

Most of all, thanks Stephanie and Caroline. I took so many moments away from you to write. Your patience and support mean the world to me.

John Pilate will return soon--as short stories, audio books, novellas and full-scale novels.

Until then, I hope you will continue to be active on our Facebook and Google+ pages. It keeps me keeping on when you pop over and say hello. Finally, your reviews on Amazon or wherever you bought this book are crucial. Please take a moment for a candid review. It helps keep the roads of Cross Township cleared of snow.

Peace.

J. Alexander Greenwood
Pilate's Blood written in Kansas City, Mo. and Laguna Beach, Ca.
2013/2014
http://www.PilatesCross.com